"Dance with me," he said.

Buck faced Terri and held out his hand.

Her lips parted, but she didn't speak as he drew her into his arms. She was a little stiff and self-conscious at first—Buck guessed she hadn't danced in a while. But as he pulled her close enough to be guided by his body, she softened against him, slipping into the beat of the music.

Her satiny cheek rested against his. He breathed her in, filling his senses with her sexy-clean, womanly aroma. Her curves skimmed his body, the contact hardening his arousal. There was no way she couldn't be feeling it. But she didn't pull away.

He'd made love to this woman, Buck reminded himself. He'd been inside her—and, damn it all, he ached to be there again. But that was the least of what he was feeling now.

How could he let her go after tonight? How could he watch her walk away, knowing that even if he saw her again, she would no longer be part of his life?

D1019138

Dear Reader,

Lucky me. I grew up with one of the most spectacular parts of the world—the red rock country of Southern Utah—right in my backyard. It was my family's playground, a place for hiking, picnics and holiday outings. Back in the day it was quiet. Now it draws visitors from all over the world. The little towns where we used to stop for lunch have become tourist meccas, growing every year.

A few years ago I made a deeper journey, a rafting trip down the Colorado River into the heart of the Grand Canyon. I have never been as tired, or as filthy, as I was after the grueling eight-hour hike from Phantom Ranch, in the canyon bottom, to the South Rim at the top. It was the adventure of a lifetime.

I've always wanted to share this beautiful country with you, my readers. So this story is my gift to you. Enjoy.

I would love hearing from any and all of you. You can contact me and learn more about my books through my website: www.elizabethlaneauthor.com.

Happy reading!

Elizabeth

ELIZABETH LANE

A LITTLE SURPRISE
FOR THE BOSS

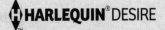

Recycling programs
for this product may
not exist in your area

ISBN-13: 978-0-373-73470-2

A Little Surprise for the Boss

Printed in U.S.A.

www.Harlequin.com

Elizabeth Lane has lived and traveled in many parts of the world, including Europe, Latin America and the Far East, but her heart remains in the American West, where she was born and raised. Her idea of heaven is hiking a mountain trail on a clear autumn day. She also enjoys music, animals and dancing. You can learn more about Elizabeth by visiting her website at www.elizabethlaneauthor.com.

Books by Elizabeth Lane

Harlequin Desire

In His Brother's Place
The Santana Heir
The Nanny's Secret
A Sinful Seduction
Stranded with the Boss
A Little Surprise for the Boss

Visit the author profile page at Harlequin.com, or elizabethlaneauthor.com, for more titles.

One

Terri Hammond dumped two aspirin into her palm and washed them down with the lukewarm coffee in her mug. The hand-thrown mug, a costly item that bore the inscription My Right-Hand Woman, had been a Christmas gift the previous December from her boss of ten years, Buck Morgan, CEO of Bucket List Enterprises. Its message, meant as a compliment, was a galling reminder of the way Buck treated her—as something that simply did whatever he asked, without requiring attention or praise. Something to be taken for granted.

To Buck's credit, he'd also given her a generous

bonus. But right now, it was all Terri could do to keep from flinging the mug against the sandstone wall of her office with all her strength.

No wonder she had a headache. It was nine forty-five, the day was already turning into the Monday from hell, and Buck was nowhere to be found.

The morning had started with a voice mail from Jay Mickleson, the instructor for the resort's scheduled afternoon skydive. He'd thrown out his back over the weekend and couldn't show up for the jump that had been booked. If Terri couldn't raise one of the other instructors or find Buck, she'd have to do the job herself. She was licensed and certified, but it was just one more thing to add to an already hectic day—a day that was just getting started.

As Terri was about to check her email, a call had come from the nursing supervisor at Canyon Shadows Assisted Living. Terri's ninety-one-year-old grandmother was refusing to eat again. When the aide had tried to feed her, the old woman swore at the poor girl, knocked the plate to the floor, and demanded that somebody be called to come and drive her home.

The incident would blow over just as they always had in the past, Terri knew. But she felt duty bound to show up. It was nobody's fault that the sweet, patient woman who'd raised her after her parents died had become erratic and miserable in her old age and dementia. Her grandmother still deserved—and needed—love and attention.

While she was waiting for Bob, her young assistant, to show up and cover the calls, the phone rang again. Terri's nerves clenched as she recognized the voice of Diane, Buck's ex-wife, who, thanks to a smart divorce lawyer, owned a 20 percent share of Bucket List Enterprises.

"Terri? Put Buck on." In Terri's experience, the word *please* had never escaped the woman's collagen-enhanced lips. Neither had *thank you*.

"Sorry, Diane, he's not here."

"Well, where is he? He's not answering his cell."

"I know. I've tried to reach him. He's not answering his landline at home, either. Can I help you with something?"

"Well…" Her tongue made a little *click*. "You can pass this on. I can't drive Quinn up there this week because I'm hosting a spiritual cleansing retreat here in Sedona. If Buck wants his daughter for the summer, he's going to have to send someone to get her or come himself."

Terri bit back a snarky retort. "I'll pass that on."

"Fine. Do that." The call ended. Terri sighed as she hung up the phone. Buck's nine-year-old daughter was a little champ. But her parents relayed her back and forth like the shuttlecock in a badminton game. Neither of them seemed to have much time for the girl.

Getting Quinn here was Buck's problem, not hers. But it was her job to let him know. She picked up the phone again and punched in his cell number. She heard the recorded answer in the deep, sexy drawl that, after all these years, still raised goose bumps on the back of her neck.

Hi. You've reached Buck Morgan. I'm not available right now. Leave a message and I'll get back to you soon as I can.

Terri waited for the beep. "Blast it, Buck, where are you? Jay hurt his back. He's probably out for the week. And you need to phone Diane about picking up Quinn in Sedona—she says she can't drive her out. Call me."

Five minutes later, Bob walked in, late as usual. Dark-haired and handsome at nineteen, he was sure of himself to the point of arrogance. But when it came to actual experience or know-how to back up his ego...he had a lot to learn. Especially when it came to running things at Bucket List Enterprises. After three weeks of struggling to train him, Terri had doubts about his willingness to learn any of it. But since his father was one of Buck's partners, she was stuck with him. She sighed as he waved a greeting. What she wouldn't give for some reliable help.

After telling him where she was going and leaving him with some brief instructions, she shoved on her sunglasses and dashed out through the rustic, open-beamed lobby of the luxury hotel that was the center of Buck's business. Her vintage Jeep was parked in the employee row, next to Bob's Corvette. Piling into the driver's seat, she swung onto Porter Hollow's main street and headed for the nursing home. Her long chestnut hair, caught back in a ponytail, waved behind her as she drove.

By the time she arrived, the crisis was over. "Harriet calmed down not long after we called you," the nursing director told her. "She finally ate some breakfast and went to sleep in her lounge chair in front of the TV."

"You're not giving her anything to make her sleep, are you?" Terri demanded.

"Of course not, dear. She's just old and tired. Any little thing wears her out these days."

Terri took the stairs to the second floor, walked down the carpeted hallway and opened the door to her grandmother's tiny studio apartment. The TV was blaring a popular game show, but the old woman wasn't watching. She lay partway back in her old leather recliner, her head sagging to one side like a tired little sparrow's as she slept. She looked so small and frail that Terri had to fight back tears.

After turning off the TV, Terri left without waking her. She would come back to visit tonight after dinner. Right now she needed to check on Buck.

Worry gnawed at her as she turned onto Main Street. Buck had worked hard to build his business, and he took a hands-on approach to running it. The other side of that was that he played as hard as he worked. Oversleeping after a wild night wasn't unheard of. But it wasn't like him to drop out of sight without telling her, or at least leaving his phone on so she could reach him. Something had to be wrong.

On this warm mid-June day, Main Street was crowded with tourists. Visitors roamed the boardwalks that lined the narrow roadway, browsing the expensive boutiques and art galleries, and eating brunch in the upscale gourmet restaurants.

For generations, Porter Hollow had been a sleepy little southern Utah town, nestled amid spectacular red rock scenery but largely undiscovered by the rest of the world. Buck, who'd grown up here, had come home from the army eleven years ago burning with ideas to bring the place to life and garner the town worldwide attention.

Starting small, he'd partnered with several outdoor-adventure companies to form Bucket List Enterprises. Within a few years the town had become a magnet for high-end adventure seekers. Porter Hollow offered access to four national parks, the vast waters of Lake Powell and the Tony Award–winning Utah Shakespeare Festival in nearby Cedar City. Buck's clients could enjoy river rafting, sport fishing, hiking, biking, skydiving, four-wheeling and horseback trips into the nearby mountains. With the construction of a sprawling luxury hotel complex, featuring exclusive shops, five-star restaurants, a spa, a beauty salon and the booking office for Bucket List Adventures, Buck had forged a kingdom. As holder of a 70 percent company share, he was its absolute ruler. Even Terri could only guess how many millions of dollars he was worth.

From the main highway, Terri took a right turn onto the road that wound two miles up a vermilion-hued canyon to the gated property where Buck had built his home. She would check there first. If she failed to find him, she would start making phone calls. Buck Morgan wasn't just her boss. The two of them went back a long way. She was genuinely concerned about him.

Growing up, Terri had known Buck as the best friend of her older brother, Steve. Buck and Steve had played football together, hunted and fished together, and double-dated the prettiest girls in school. After graduation, the two of them had joined the army and deployed in the same unit. Buck had survived Iraq and made it home without a scratch. Steve had been shot dead on patrol and come home to Porter Hollow in a flag-draped coffin. His death had devastated Terri. But Buck had tried to make sure she was all right. When, after two years of college, she'd returned home to care for her aging grandmother, he'd offered her a well-paying job as his assistant and office manager. Working side by side, her feelings for him had only grown—not that he'd ever seemed to notice. Buck had been a loyal friend to her, but it had always been clear that friendship was the only relationship he wanted with her, despite his affairs with an endless string of women.

Her grandmother's declining health, and her loyalty to Buck, had kept Terri in Porter Hollow and with Bucket List Enterprises for the past ten years. But recently she'd begun to question her future. She was thirty years old. Did she really want to spend her life looking after a man with a weakness for sexy blondes—a man who never gave her a second look, except when he needed something done?

It wasn't as if she didn't have options. As Buck's assistant, she'd gotten to know the owners of other resorts in the region. Several had expressed an interest in poaching her. Moving her grandmother shouldn't be a problem. There had to be nice facilities in other towns—some of them better than Canyon Shadows.

She should give it some serious thought, Terri told herself as she drove up the canyon. A change of scene might be good for her. It might even help her get over the flaming crush she'd had on Buck Morgan since she was fourteen.

Pulling up to the wrought iron gate, Terri entered the code on the keypad. She felt a prickle of nervous apprehension. What would she find when she reached the house? What could explain Buck's mysterious silence?

A symphony of stone, wood and glass, the house was set amid cliffs and massive boulders like part of the landscape. The interior featured soaring cathedral ceilings and a huge stone fireplace. Buck could easily have afforded servants, but he liked his privacy. He made do with a weekly cleaning crew from the hotel to keep the place spotless.

The place looked undisturbed. As Terri pulled into the driveway, she could see Murphy, Buck's big rescue mutt, romping in the enclosed part of the yard. An imposing mix of rottweiler and pit bull, he was as playful and affectionate as he was scary-looking. He bounded up to the tall fence, tongue lolling and tail wagging, as she climbed out of the Jeep.

"Hello, boy." Terri stuck her fingers through the chain links so the dog could slurp them. The dog didn't seem upset—which he'd likely be if something was wrong. And Buck's tan Hummer was parked outside the garage, which meant he was most likely here. But if he was here, why wasn't he answering either of his phones?

The door swung open to a silent house. No TV. No sounds or smells from the kitchen. She checked the kitchen and dining room, the pantry, the den, and the downstairs bathroom. Aside from a single coffee cup and a spoon in the sink, there was no sign of life. The bedrooms, including Buck's, were upstairs. Cringing inside, Terri crept up the open staircase. What if Buck was here and he had company? If she heard telltale noises coming from his bedroom, she'd be out of the house faster than a scared jackrabbit.

From the landing, she could see that the door to Buck's room was partway open. Peeking around the door frame, she saw that the blinds were drawn, the room dim and quiet. Finally she could make out a solitary figure sprawled facedown in the rumpled king-size bed—sheets twisted around long, bare legs, a smudge of dark hair against the pillow. It was definitely Buck. But was he all right? It wasn't like him to be in bed at this hour on a workday.

Shedding her sandals in the hall, she tiptoed into the room. She could hear the deep rasp of his breathing. At least he was alive. Edging closer, she could see his shoes and work clothes scattered on the sheepskin rug, as if he'd just peeled everything off and collapsed into bed. He wasn't even wearing…

Heat rushed to Terri's face as her gaze fixed on the twin moons of his rump, nicely framed by a fold of the twisted sheet. The man wasn't wearing a stitch. What she could see of him looked damned good.

But this was no time to ogle her boss's scrumptious body. Something here wasn't right. He was either sick or drugged, maybe both.

His cell phone was on the nightstand, switched off. She also noticed an empty water glass and two plastic prescription bottles. Holding them to the light from the hall, she inspected the labels. One she recognized as a heavy-duty analgesic Buck took for his occasional migraines. The other was unfamiliar. But if Buck had taken them in combination, the side effects could have knocked him out—or worse.

She was no doctor. But one thing was certain. She couldn't just walk away and leave him like this. She needed to wake him up and make sure he was all right.

Reluctant to startle him, she nudged his bare shoulder. "Buck, wake up," she whispered.

A quiver passed through his body. He groaned, the sound muffled by the pillow.

"Wake up, Buck! Open your eyes!" She shook his shoulder again, harder this time. He moaned, twitched and rolled over onto his back. His stunning cobalt eyes were open, but they had a glazed, drowsy look.

"Hullo, pretty lady," he muttered. "You showed up just in time."

"In time for what?" Terri asked. Buck appeared to be half-asleep. He didn't even seem to recognize her. "Pretty lady" was his usual term of endearment for his conquests—he'd never called her that before.

"For this." He clasped her wrist and trailed her hand down his belly under the tangled sheet. Gently but firmly he folded her fingers around a stallion-sized erection.

Terri's heart lurched. She was no virgin—she'd had a couple of relationships in college and a short-lived fling on a trip to Hawaii. But that had been a long time ago, and this was *Buck*, not only her boss, but her friend—and the man she'd secretly pined over for years.

Clearly he wasn't in his right mind. If she was smart, she'd slap him back to his senses and leave. But the heat was already pounding through her body. Even after he released her wrist, she couldn't make her fingers let go of that warm, silky, amazing hardness.

Heaven help her, she *wanted* him.

"C'mere, you…" he said, while she was still trying to convince herself that she should, she *must* leave. Hand catching the back of her head, he pulled her down for a rough, possessive kiss that pushed every sensible logical thought out of her mind. His tongue invaded her mouth, stroking and teasing the sensitive surfaces. Desire blazed through her like the flame of a blowtorch. She could feel the wetness as her body prepared to welcome him. Common sense took flight.

She wanted him so much. And it felt so incredible to believe, in this moment, that he wanted her, too.

His hands, deft and practiced, unfastened her khakis and slid them down her legs, along with her panties. Shifting on the bed, he encouraged her to straddle him, positioning her body on top of his. He slid his hand between her legs, and she could feel his grin against her lips at the wetness he found.

She leaned over him, clasped his hips with her knees and eased herself down onto his shaft. Her eyes closed as he slid upward, completely filling her. He groaned in satisfaction as her lips parted, her breath sucked inward. This was Buck inside her—the man she'd wanted from the time she'd learned what sex was all about. Even the thought was enough to trigger the delicious little spasm of her first climax.

She began to move, taking the time at first to feel every inch of him gliding in and out of her. Then, for both of them, urgency took over. His breath deepened, hips arching to meet her as she pushed harder, faster, until with a groan he rolled her onto her back, moved on top of her and took charge.

Her legs wound around his hips as he thrust into her, driving like a bull, until she burst with him, clenching around him in a climax that fulfilled fifteen years of fantasies.

With a grunt of satisfaction, he rolled off her and lay back on the pillow. For a few seconds Terri was still, basking in the afterglow. Then reality fell on her with a crash. She'd just had mindless, gasket-blowing sex with her boss. Nothing would ever be the same between them again.

Sitting up, she gazed down at him. Buck's eyes were closed, his breathing deep and even. His face wore a contented little smirk.

The man had gone back to sleep—if he'd ever actually been fully awake.

Her face burned as the truth sank home. The earth might have moved for her. But what about him? He'd roused to find a woman in his bedroom and simply reacted. She could have been anyone. When he woke up later, the odds were he'd only barely remember this encounter. She wasn't at all sure he'd remember that the woman had been her.

That would be for the best, Terri told herself as she slipped off the bed and gathered her clothes without disturbing him. If Buck didn't remember the identity of his mystery lover, there'd be no awkwardness, no embarrassing confrontations—and of course, she'd never tell him. They could go on as before, as if nothing had happened.

Or…could this be the thing she'd been looking for, to shake up her life from the rut it was in?

Dare she hope that this would change things between them? That he would look at her and see the warm, loving—and sexy, damn it—woman behind the loyal assistant who'd been at his side like a faithful hound for the past ten years?

If not, maybe it really was time to move on.

Before leaving the room, she switched on his cell

phone and turned the ring volume all the way up. If Diane had something to discuss, or if there was an emergency at work, he was damned well fit to answer the call.

In the hallway, she scrambled into her clothes, cramming her shirttail into her khakis and hooking the belt with shaking hands. The memory of her time in Buck's bed already felt like some kind of crazy dream. It would be up to Buck to decide whether or not to make it real.

Downstairs, she fed the dog and changed his water. Then she left. She was no longer worried about Buck's condition. He'd given her ample proof that he was going to be fine. She would go back to work and let him sleep off whatever was in his system. Meanwhile, there were plenty of other things to demand her attention.

Twenty minutes after leaving Buck's place, she pulled into the hotel parking lot, switched off the Jeep's ignition and took a moment to compose herself. Her pulse was still racing at the memory of the time she'd spent in his bed. When she'd driven to his canyon home, the last thing she'd expected was to sleep with the man. Getting back to normal was going to be a challenge. And she couldn't repress the surge of excitement at the thought that they might be on the verge of a *new* normal.

But until then, she had to pull herself together. Glancing down, she smoothed her khaki shirt with the Bucket List logo on the front pocket, then climbed out of the vehicle and strode across the parking lot to the hotel entrance.

The hotel lobby was a showplace. Built in rustic style, like the lodges at the nearby Grand Canyon, it featured walls of red sandstone slabs, massive open-beam construction and a slate floor. At the far end, a stone fireplace rose to the ceiling. Between the entrance and the front desk, a waterfall cascaded down a face of natural rock. Exquisite Navajo rugs hung on the walls, and the gift shops sold real Native American textiles, jewelry and pottery. There was no tourist junk. Buck had insisted that everything sold here be not only authentic but of gallery quality.

Terri smiled a greeting to the clerks as she passed the front desk, then darted down a hallway to the women employees' restroom. When she checked herself in the mirror, she expected to see her usual ordinary features—the copper-flecked brown eyes and no-nonsense brows, the square chin, the straight nose sprinkled with freckles, all arranged into the business-like expression she wore at work. But the face gazing back at her was almost a stranger's—cheeks flushed, moist lips swollen, eyes large and bright in a surprisingly sensual face. Nobody who saw her could help but notice the difference.

Good grief! Why not simply hang a sign around her neck reading I Just Had Hot Sex with the Boss?

With a shake of her head, she turned on the cold water, splashed her face and blotted it dry with a paper towel. Slicking her lips with the colored gloss she carried in her purse and smoothing her hair back with her damp hands, she called it good. Duty awaited.

The booking and management office for Bucket List Adventures was down the hall in its own wing of the hotel complex. It consisted of an open area for the staff, break and conference rooms, restrooms, a modest office for Terri, and a spacious office for Buck.

Terri breezed in from the covered hallway that connected with the hotel, trying to look as if nothing had happened. She found Bob in her office, sitting back in her chair with his boots on her desk and spilled coffee leaving a trail across the mahogany surface. A spark of annoyance flared. But she bit back a sharp comment. She'd asked the boy to cover the phones. He probably didn't know how to transfer the calls to his own desk.

"So catch me up," she said. "What's happening?"

Making no move to get out of her chair, though he did at least have the grace to drop his feet off the desk and look a bit embarrassed, he picked up a yellow notepad. At least he knew enough to write down messages. "The skydive's covered," he said. "Jay called another instructor who was willing to take it."

"That's a relief." And it was. After this morning, she was in no condition to parachute out of a plane with the seventy-year-old woman who was jumping to celebrate her birthday. "Anything else?" she asked.

"Diane called again. She wanted to know where Buck was. I told her you'd gone to look for him." He glanced up at her. "Did you have any luck?"

Terri willed her expression to freeze. "Buck isn't feeling well. He'd turned off his phone so he could get some rest, that's all."

"Well, I guess I should give you your desk back." He stood then, a gangly figure who towered over Terri by a head. "Hey, did you lose your earring?" he asked.

"Oh!" Terri's hands went to her earlobes. One earring was in place. The other was missing.

The little turquoise-inlaid silver earrings in the shape of Kokopelli, the Native American flute-playing deity, were her favorite pair. She'd received a lot of compliments on them. Even Buck had noticed them.

The missing earring could have fallen off anywhere. But it hadn't. Terri's gut feeling told her exactly how and where she'd lost it.

Buck would be sure to recognize it. And that meant that he'd have to acknowledge what had occurred between them. Her stomach roiled in fear and anticipation. This could be a disaster…or it could be the start of something amazing. And she had no way of knowing which until Buck finally arrived.

Two

Buck's ringing cell phone blasted him out of a sound sleep. Cursing, he fumbled for the device on the nightstand and sent it clattering to the floor.

Damn! He could've sworn he'd turned that phone off before collapsing into bed last night. And he would *never* set the ringer up to its full, earsplitting volume. What the devil was going on?

Grabbing the phone from the floor, he pushed the answer button. "Hullo?" he mumbled.

"Where've you been, Buck?" As always, Diane's voice scraped his nerves like fingernails on a chalkboard. The worst of it was, between the daughter they shared and the chunk of his company she owned, he'd likely be hearing that shrill voice for the rest of his life.

"Sick." He forced the word through a throat that felt as if he'd swallowed glue.

"Well, get unsick. It's almost noon. Did you get my voice-mail messages? I must've left you three or four."

"Haven't checked."

"I'll save you the trouble—I need you to pick up Quinn."

His daughter's name jarred him to alertness. "Weren't you supposed to bring her here?"

"I've got people coming for a retreat. I could bring her up next week, but she's all packed and ready to go. If she has to wait, she'll be *so* disappointed."

"Fine. I'll send Evie Redfeather down in the jet to pick her up." Evie was his personal pilot. Quinn knew and liked her.

"You can't come yourself?"

"Like you, I have other commitments. Tell her Evie's coming. She'll be fine with that." Buck ended the call before Diane could think of some other way to pull his strings. This last-minute change of plans was typical. Diane would have known about her retreat for weeks and could have made arrangements for Quinn earlier. But why do that when she could create a little drama?

Diane had been a Vegas showgirl when he'd met her ten years ago. After a hot weekend in her bed, he'd flown home without giving her a second thought. But then she'd shown up pregnant on his doorstep, and he'd done the honorable thing. For a while they'd tried to make the marriage work, but it had been doomed from the first "I do." After a nightmare divorce settlement, she'd moved to Sedona, Arizona, and opened her own new age ashram.

The experience had left Buck with a bitter taste when it came to marriage. But at least he had Quinn. Quinn had been worth it all.

The phone shrilled again. Knowing it was Diane, Buck turned it off and lay back on the pillow. He'd come home last night with a pounding migraine. Feeling like roadkill, he'd taken some pills, undressed and fallen into bed, hoping to sleep through the pain. It had worked. He felt better today.

Especially after that crazy, sexy dream he'd had.

Closing his eyes, he tried to recall it in detail. He'd had erotic dreams before, plenty of them, but this one had been different. It had seemed so...*real*. The warm silkiness of skin against his body. The taste of that luscious mouth. Even the sexy aroma of her skin. He could remember everything about the woman—except her face.

Damn! He'd gulp down a whole bottle of those blasted pills if it could bring the dream back. His climax had been an explosion of sheer sensual pleasure, so powerful he'd probably drenched the bedding underneath him.

He frowned, struck by an odd notion. He should be lying in a damp spot now. But the sheet beneath him felt perfectly clean and dry.

Perplexed, he sat up, moved to one side and ran his hand across the mattress. Nothing. He shook his head, as if trying to clear out the cobwebs. What in blazes had happened here?

That was when he noticed something else—a subtle fragrance rising from the bottom sheet. Pressing his face to the fabric, he inhaled the sweet, clean aroma, trying to identify it. This wasn't the softener the hotel laundry used. And it wasn't one of the expensive perfumes his sexual partners tended to drench themselves in. It was something else, something fresh but somehow familiar. It was *her* scent, exactly as he remembered it.

There could be only one conclusion—the dream had been real. There'd been a woman in his bed, and he'd made love to her.

But how could that be? There'd been no one here when he'd gone to bed last night. The gate to the property had been locked. The house had been locked. And if the dog had barked at an intruder, he hadn't heard it.

Was he losing his mind?

He sat up. The room looked the same as usual. Nothing appeared to have been touched except—

His gaze fell on the phone.

Now that his head was clearing, he distinctly recalled turning it off before he went to sleep. But someone had not only turned it on again but adjusted the ring volume loud enough to raise the dead.

Who would play such a dirty trick on him?

Maybe he was *still* dreaming.

Sliding his legs off the bed, he pushed to his feet and stood on the sheepskin rug. His legs felt as shaky

as Jell-O, probably because the pills hadn't worn off.
Maybe if he went downstairs and got some coffee in
his system, he'd be able to think straight.

His robe was draped over the foot of the bed. He
took a step toward it, then jerked back with a grunt
of pain. His bare foot had come down on something
sharp—some object caught in the thick wool of the
rug.

Bending over, he found it with his fingers, picked
it up and held it to the light. It was a small silver earring, inlaid with turquoise and fashioned in the shape
of Kokopelli, the humpbacked Native American flute
player. He stared at it, recognition slamming him like
a mule kick.

Terri's earring.

Buck sank onto the edge of the bed. Lord, could
he have had mind-blowing sex with *Terri*, who'd always been like a kid sister to him? *Terri*, that mir-
acle of patience and efficiency who kept the hectic
world of Bucket List Enterprises running like well-
oiled clockwork?

No, it was unbelievable. But it was the only possible
answer. Terri would have the gate code and the security combination for the front door. The dog, who'd
bark at any stranger, knew her well. Glancing at the
clock, he saw how late he'd slept. That made sense,
too—Terri must have come to check on him when he
hadn't shown up at work.

And only Terri would have turned on his cell phone
when she left and set the ringer loud enough to wake

him. Knowing her, she probably would've fed the dog, too. He would remember to check when he went downstairs.

But if Terri was the answer, he still had plenty of questions. Had he really had sex with her? But the dream, which seemed less and less dreamlike the more he thought of it, left little doubt of that. He remembered waking up to a woman leaning over him, remembered pulling her into bed. Remembered her response, and the way she'd made him feel… He'd initiated the encounter, but she'd come willingly.

No way would she have joined him in that bed… unless she'd wanted to.

Holding that thought, Buck showered in the bathroom, finger-raked his hair, and pulled on sweatpants and a T-shirt. He was wide-awake now, but going back to work today wouldn't be a great idea, especially since Terri would be there. Sooner or later he'd have to face her. But before that happened, he had some serious thinking to do.

He took a minute to phone Evie Redfeather and arrange for her to pick up Quinn in Sedona. Evie, a retired air force fighter pilot, had made the short flight before and said she didn't mind going again. That taken care of, he went downstairs in his bare feet to make coffee.

With cup in hand he wandered out onto the redwood deck and leaned on the railing. His eyes traced the passing flight of a golden eagle, its wings casting a brief shadow against the sunset-hued cliffs. A downward glance into the yard confirmed that Murphy's food dish was full of kibble, his water bowl freshly filled. Terri had been here, all right. No one else would think to take care of his dog while he was sick.

But what was he going to do about her? Terri was his right-hand woman, the person he depended on for everything from booking tours and flights to hiring and firing employees to fending off Diane. But sleeping with her would change the dynamics of what had been a perfect relationship—a relationship he couldn't afford to lose. He could get a bed partner anytime he wanted one. But, damn it, Terri was irreplaceable.

Buck sipped his coffee and thought hard. This misstep would have to be dealt with. The question was, how?

He could call her into his office—no, maybe take her out to dinner, apologize profusely and promise it would never happen again. But how might Terri respond to that? At best it would create an awkward situation between them. Or she could be hurt. She could feel rejected, even angry. She could even—God forbid—quit her job and leave.

There had to be a way to put this behind them without harming their relationship.

Buck gazed down at the cooled dregs of the coffee in his cup, thinking hard. What if he were to behave as if the whole thing had never happened? After all, he'd been half-asleep. Surely Terri wouldn't be surprised if he didn't remember. She might even be relieved.

The more he thought about the idea the better it

sounded. Nothing would have to change—no expectations, no awkwardness. Terri could go on working for him as always. Even if she suspected him of knowing, she'd have no proof.

His white lie would save face for both of them.

But it didn't make him feel any better about what had happened. Sex with Terri had been sensational. With any other woman, he would have been lobbying for a return engagement. But Terri was off-limits. Not only was she his employee but she was Steve's kid sister, the girl he'd promised to look after when Steve didn't make it home from Iraq.

And having half-drugged sex with her wasn't part of that promise.

At the moment Buck didn't like himself much. Between now and the next time he saw her, he had some soul-searching to do.

By the time Terri had finished her last task for the day—posting tomorrow's schedule online—it was an hour past closing time. Bob and the summer temps had gone, leaving her there alone to close up. She was about to lock the door when Quinn, trailed by Evie Redfeather, came bounding across the parking lot.

"Hi, Terri!" Blond ponytail flying, Quinn collided with Terri in an exuberant hug.

Terri hugged her back. She adored Buck's daughter. "How's my favorite girl?" she asked, meaning it.

"Great!" Quinn's blue eyes, so like her father's, sparkled.

"You're taller," Terri said.

"I know. Mom says I'm having a growth spurt. The clothes I left here won't fit. We'll have to go shopping for new ones."

Evie Redfeather had come up behind her. In her early fifties, she was a handsome, broad-faced Navajo woman. "Buck asked me to drop her off at his house, but we were two hours late getting out of Sedona." She shook her head. "That woman! Always with the drama!"

Terri didn't have to ask Evie who she meant.

"I saw your Jeep in the parking lot and realized you must still be here," Evie said. "I hope you won't mind running Quinn home. Bert and I are expecting friends for dinner. I need to get going."

"Sure." Terri stifled a groan. The last thing she wanted was to show up at Buck's house with Quinn. The conversation they needed to have couldn't happen with little ears present. "Go on, Evie. Thanks for picking her up."

"No problem. Here, I've got her bag. I'll put it in your Jeep."

Terri felt Quinn's hand slip into hers as they followed Evie's long strides to the Jeep. She fought back a rising attack of nerves. How would Buck react to what had happened? Would he treat her any differently because of it? Would he be embarrassed? Aloof? Indifferent?

But this wasn't about her and Buck, Terri reminded herself. It was about Quinn, and making the little girl's homecoming a happy occasion. She could only hope Buck would be out of bed and fit to welcome his daughter.

"Up you go." She boosted Quinn into the high seat of the Jeep. "Hang on, we'll have you there in a jiffy."

"What's a jiffy?" Quinn asked as Terri climbed into the Jeep. "You use the funniest words, Terri."

"A jiffy is a very short bit of time. I learned lots of old-fashioned words from my grandma. Maybe I should've said we'd be there in the flick of a lamb's tail. Would you have liked that better?"

Quinn giggled. Terri had kept her distance during the short duration of Buck's marriage. But after the divorce, once Quinn became old enough to spend time in Utah with her father, she'd become attached to the little girl. Maybe too attached. What if Buck were to remarry? Could she back off and let Quinn go?

But she wouldn't think about that now. Things were already complicated enough.

"Can we go out for pizza tonight?" Quinn asked. "I want lots of pepperoni on mine. Mom's vegan now, so she won't let me eat meat. She didn't even give me a choice."

"Don't they make vegan pepperoni?"

"It's yucky. So's the cheese. Has Dad got a new girlfriend yet? I didn't like the last one. She was scared of bugs and she was always fixing her makeup."

"I don't know," Terri said. "You'll have to ask him. And you can ask him about the pizza, too. He's your parent. I'm not."

"You sound mad. Are you mad, Terri?"

"At you? No way!" Terri reached across the seat and squeezed the girl's shoulder. She'd have to watch herself around Quinn. The perceptive child was wise beyond her years. If she sensed any tension where Buck was concerned, she was apt to ask awkward questions.

They'd turned off the main road and were headed up the canyon. Terri felt the knot tighten in the pit of her stomach as she realized she was still wearing her single Kokopelli earring. Had Buck found its mate in his bedroom? Or had he not yet left the bed where she'd left him, after the most explosive sexual experience of her life?

They swung up the private road to the gate, and Terri punched in the code. Buck would surely know his daughter was coming. At least he'd been awake enough to have Evie fly down and pick her up. But just to avoid an unpleasant surprise, she pushed the intercom button.

"Hi." His deep baritone went through her with the shock of memory. It made her shiver to realize she now knew exactly how that voice sounded sex-drenched and husky.

"It's me." The words emerged as nervous squeaks. "I'm bringing Quinn."

"Great. Come on up." His voice betrayed nothing. Either he was a good actor or he wasn't ready to talk about what had happened in his bedroom.

Or he didn't care. Knowing Buck, that was possible, too.

* * *

Buck stood on the front porch watching the Jeep come up the drive. Seeing Terri was a surprise. He'd asked Evie to bring Quinn here. But there must've been a change of plans.

Things could be awkward with Terri. He didn't quite know what to expect from her. But Quinn would be with them. That would make things all right—for now, at least.

The Jeep pulled up next to his Hummer and stopped. Throwing off her seat belt, Quinn bounded out of the passenger seat and raced up the steps to give him a hug. As he swung her off her feet, he could tell she'd grown since Christmas break. With her in Sedona most of the year, he was missing so much of her life. Maybe this summer he could find a way to spend more time with her.

"Hi, Daddy," she said. "I missed you."

"Me, too." He lowered her to the ground. "Are you hungry?"

"Starved."

"She told me she wanted pizza." Terri had come up the steps with Quinn's suitcase. Buck looked at her and forced a smile. Terri smiled back at him, but her eyes held a flicker of uncertainty. She was wearing one of her Kokopelli earrings. Her other earlobe was bare.

That clinched it. If Buck had had any doubt about her being in his bed this morning, it was totally gone.

He was still dealing with the reality of it. Terri was

an attractive woman—beautiful in an unassuming way. But he'd always made it a rule to keep his hands off his best friend's sister. Steve had been gone for a dozen years now, but that rule hadn't changed. Until now, he'd assumed she had the same rule. But this morning had thrown the rule book out the window, for both of them.

He forced himself up to speak. "Pizza it is. How about Giovanni's?"

"Yes!" Quinn grinned. "Their pizza's the yummiest! Can Terri come with us?"

"Terri?" He looked at her, half hoping she'd make an excuse not to come along. Terri's presence was rousing his memory and putting lustful thoughts into his head—the last thing he needed right now. Their interlude this morning had been incredible...but it could never be repeated.

"I'd better not," she said, avoiding his eyes. "I promised my grandmother I'd come and visit her tonight."

"Please, Terri!" Quinn begged. "If we go now you'll still have time to see your grandma."

"Come on, Terri." Buck remembered his resolve to act as if nothing had happened. "It won't be a party without you."

She hesitated, then sighed. "All right. I *am* getting hungry. But let me follow you in the Jeep. That way, when we're finished, I can just go from Giovanni's to Canyon Shadows."

"Okay. Let's get going." Buck put Quinn's bag inside the house and helped her into the passenger seat of the Hummer. He had to believe that in time, if he kept up the act, things would go back to normal. But right now, with the memory of Terri's lithe, lush body fresh in his mind, it was like walking a tightrope over a volcano. One slip and he'd be in big trouble.

Terri waited until the Hummer had backed down the steep driveway. Then she turned the Jeep around and followed the hulking vehicle down to the road. It wasn't too late to head off in a different direction. She could always make an excuse, call Buck's cell, apologize and say that she'd remembered an important errand. But Quinn would be disappointed if she didn't show up to share a pizza. Buck, on the other hand, didn't seem to care either way—about sharing a pizza with her now, or about sharing a bed with her this morning.

Part of her wanted to believe that this morning would make a difference, that Buck would look at her and see a warm, desirable woman. But clearly that hadn't happened. It was time for her to face the truth. No matter what happened, Buck was never going to see her the way she wanted to be seen. There was only one question left: What was she going to do about it?

Twilight was settling over the town and over the sandstone cliffs that ringed it like the setting of a jewel. Main Street glittered with streams of traffic. Shoppers and diners strolled the boardwalks. Music drifted from cafés and taverns.

This was Buck's town, but that didn't mean she had to stay here forever. She had the qualifications and the experience to get a job anywhere in the tourist industry. She'd be a fool to let loyalty keep her in a situation where she felt like a piece of furniture.

Giovanni's Pizzeria was at the far end of Main Street. When the Hummer's taillights turned into the parking lot, Terri followed and pulled into the next space. Buck and Quinn were waiting for her when she climbed out of the Jeep. "Let's go!" Quinn seized her hand and pulled her toward the entrance. "Extralarge pepperoni and giant root beer, here I come!"

Buck chuckled as he caught up with Terri. "Quinn tells me her mother's had her on nothing but wheatgrass juice and tofu," he said. "She's probably exaggerating, but it'll be a pleasure to see her enjoy real food."

Terri forced a little laugh. The hostess showed them to a booth with a traditional red-checked tablecloth and a candle melting down the outside of an empty wine bottle. They slid into the seats, Terri and Quinn on one side, Buck on the other. Their waitress came right over to take their order. The pretty blonde was a stranger to Terri, but she seemed to know Buck.

"So this is your little girl!" She flashed a toothpaste-ad smile. "What's her name?"

Buck, all charm, made the introductions. "Jennifer, this is Quinn. And this lady—" He gave Terri a nod. "This is Terri, my right-hand woman."

Terri forced a friendly smile. Inside, she was seething. Why couldn't Buck have used her job title, or just her name? Didn't he know how demeaning *right-hand woman* sounded? Obviously not, unless it was meant as hidden message to the waitress—*don't worry, she's not my girlfriend.*

Meanwhile, the waitress was looking at Buck as if she wanted to eat him alive. No doubt she'd be happy to sleep with him, if she hadn't already.

Terri brought herself up with a mental slap. Good Lord, she couldn't be jealous! Buck had never tried to hide his love life from her. She'd always accepted his shenanigans with a sisterly shrug, burying any hurt bone-deep. Even his shotgun marriage hadn't shaken her unconditional affection for the man. And she certainly hadn't expected for Buck to promise her fidelity and exclusivity after one romp in the bedroom together. But to see him now, just hours after their encounter, flirting with another woman while treating her with his usual indifference, she felt a senseless urge to leap across the table and smack Buck's handsome face.

Grow up and get over it! she told herself as the petite blonde walked away from the table with their order. Even the sway of her jeans-clad hips held an invitation. The art of seduction was one Terri had never mastered. And suddenly she felt very insecure about her performance that morning. She was hardly the alluring, experienced type of woman he usually chose as a bedmate. The sex had seemed fantastic to her… but had it been merely forgettable to him?

She had to forget what had happened. That would be the only way to survive life in Buck's magnetic aura. That—or leave.

Quinn's happy chatter was enough to fill the awkward silence while they waited for their order. Lost in her own thoughts, Terri was startled when Buck reached across the table and nudged her arm. "Hey," he said, "where have you gone to?"

She blinked herself back to the present. "Did you need something?" she asked.

He gave a shake of his head. "You're not at work now, Terri. I don't need anything. I just asked you a question. Did you know one of your earrings was missing?"

"Oh, yes." Reflexively, she brushed a hand to her bare earlobe. Was it an innocent question, or was he testing her? "Bob noticed it was gone earlier today. I'm still hoping it'll turn up somewhere."

"Too bad. I know you liked that pair." His expression was all innocence.

"Yes, I did." Terri scrambled to change the subject. "Quinn was telling me she's growing out of her clothes. I think she needs a shopping trip."

"I'll let you off early tomorrow to take her," he said. "Take my credit card and get her anything she wants."

"Can I have an iguana?" Quinn asked.

Buck raised an eyebrow. "Now where did *that* come from?"

"My friend has one. It's really cool. I'd take care of it. Iguanas are easy. They just eat lettuce and stuff."

"Think about it a minute," Buck said. "If it eats, it poops. You'd have to clean its cage every day. Could you do that?"

"Sure. That stuff doesn't bother me."

"But what would you do with it at the end of the summer?" Terri put in. "You can't just walk away from an animal and leave it here. You'd have to take it home with you. Would your mother let you keep it?"

"If I ask her and she says yes, can I have one?"

"Ask her first. Then we'll talk about it." Buck cast Terri a grateful glance. He ran Bucket List with an iron hand, but his daughter could talk him into anything—whether it was a good idea or not.

What the little girl really wanted was his time. But it was easier for him to flash his credit card and get her whatever caught her eye. By now Terri knew the pattern. Now that she had arrived for the summer, Buck would welcome Quinn with open arms—he did love his child. But as business issues pulled him away, she'd be shunted off to riding and swimming lessons, turned over to Terri, or left to read books or play video games on her own. Maybe this summer, Terri could help her find some friends her own age in the area.

The subject of the iguana was tabled when the pizza and drinks arrived. Terri tried to ignore the way Jennifer's hip brushed Buck's shoulder as she set their order on the table. Was the woman angling for a big tip or something else? But what did it matter to her? Why should she even care?

They were all hungry. Conversation dwindled as

they wolfed down the pizza. Buck had just paid the bill when Terri glanced at her watch. It was almost eight o'clock. The aides at Canyon Shadows usually came in around eight thirty to shower the residents and get them ready for bed by nine. With the facility at the far end of town from the restaurant, she would barely have time to make the promised visit to her grandmother.

She stood up, brushing the crumbs off her lap. "I've got to get going, or I won't make it."

Buck rose. "We're ready to go, too. We'll walk you out."

They trailed outside. At this hour the summer twilight was still fading. Mourning doves called from the old cottonwoods that overhung the parking lot.

"Thanks. See you tomorrow." Terri strode ahead to her Jeep, then halted with a groan. She wasn't going anywhere. The Jeep's rear tire was flat to the rim.

Three

Terri was staring at her Jeep when Buck caught up with her. "Too bad," he said. "I told you those old tires of yours needed replacing."

"Well, I can't do much about that now, can I?" Terri shook her head. Even if she left her vehicle and walked to Canyon Shadows, there was no way she'd get there in time to visit her grandmother. "Go on and take Quinn home. I know how to change a tire."

"Well, you're not doing it tonight. I've got people for that job." He whipped out his cell and, before Terri could stop him, typed out a text message before he pocketed the phone again. "Quinn and I will take you to see your grandma. I remember Harriet from the old days. She was quite the spunky little lady. I'd enjoy visiting her, too."

If Buck hadn't seen Harriet since the old days, he was in for a shock, Terri thought. Her grandmother was a different person now. "Thanks, I'd appreciate that," she said. "But you won't need to come inside. Just let me off and go. When I'm through visiting, I can walk back here and change the tire."

"You heard me—the tire will be taken care of. It's arranged. Come on." He guided her toward the Hummer with a light hand on the small of her back. The warm pressure of his palm triggered a tingle of memory that raced like flame along a fuse through her body. The feeling was sweet torture. If only she could forget what had happened between them, or at least dismiss it—as, it seemed, Buck had. But Quinn was with them now, Terri reminded herself. She wouldn't know for sure whether he was going to bring up what had happened between them until she was alone with him.

He opened the passenger door for her and helped Quinn into the backseat. The drive to Canyon Shadows took only a few minutes. "You don't have to stay—I really don't mind walking back to Giovanni's," Terri said as the Hummer pulled into the parking lot.

"Will you stop arguing with me, Terri?" Buck's voice carried a hint of reined impatience. "I told you, I'd be glad to come in and say hello to your grandmother. And Quinn won't mind coming in, either."

"I know that," Terri said. "It's just that my grandma has changed a lot since you knew her. She's ninety-one and not doing very well. She has her good days and bad. I've learned not to expect too much, but I worry that seeing her might upset Quinn."

He stopped the vehicle and laid a hand on her shoulder. "Let me be the judge of that, Terri," he said.

Buck had never been beyond the front doorway of Canyon Shadows. The rambling two-story stuccoed building was decent for a nursing home, with manicured grounds and a covered walkway leading to the front doors. Bouquets of silk roses and framed landscape prints cheered the lobby, but an air of gloom still hung over the place. Maybe that was inevitable when nobody who lived here wanted to be here.

He let Terri lead the way as they signed in at the front desk and continued on to the elevator and up to the second floor. In all the busy years she'd worked for him, he could barely recall asking her how her grandmother was doing. What had brought on this sudden interest in her life outside work?

But he knew the answer to that question, and it didn't make him feel proud of himself.

Eleven years ago, in an army medical tent, he'd knelt next to Steve's bed and promised his dying friend that he'd look after his kid sister. Buck had viewed giving Terri a job as the first step in keeping that promise. But over the years, as the pressures of building his business had closed in, she'd proven so capable and so willing that the focus had shifted. Instead of what he could do for her, it had become what *she* could do for *him*.

But that had never included her sharing his bed.

After finding her earring in his rug, his first thought had been how to avoid losing her help. But as the afternoon had worn on, his musings had deepened. He'd taken a long look at himself in the mirror and seen a first-class jerk looking back at him.

Steve, if he'd been here, would have punched him black and blue.

Somehow, he had to do a better job of keeping his promise. And he absolutely had to forget about taking her to bed again. As wonderful as it had been, he knew that a romantic relationship with Terri could never work. She was the kind of woman who would demand full honesty from her lover…and that was something he couldn't offer. Not with the secret he'd kept from her all this time.

If she knew the truth about what happened with Steve, she'd never let him touch her again—not even as a friend.

Her friendship was something he had to keep, not just for Steve's sake but for his own, too. She meant far too much to him for him to be willing to let her slip away. So that meant finding a way to make amends, to show her how much she meant to him—in a purely platonic way. But with a strong, independent woman like Terri, knowing where to start with winning her over wouldn't be easy—especially after what had happened this morning.

"Come on, Daddy!" Quinn tugged at him, and he realized he'd fallen behind. Terri had already opened a door partway down the long corridor and stepped into the room. Still holding Quinn's hand, he reached the doorway and paused on the threshold.

In the light of a single table lamp, the woman in the worn leather recliner looked as if a strong breath could blow out her life like a candle flame. Her face was as wrinkled as a walnut, her hair like white spider webbing on her ancient head. He would never have recognized feisty Harriet Cooper, Steve and Terri's maternal grandmother, who'd raised them after their parents died. Remorse crept over him. How many times in the old days had he been in her home and eaten at her table? And now—damn it all, he'd barely been aware that she was here. He certainly hadn't taken the time to visit.

"Hello, Grandma." Terri knelt next to the chair, the lamplight falling on her face. "I came by this morning but you were asleep," she said.

The old woman huffed, refusing to look at her.

"I'm sorry," Terri said. "I came as soon as I could."

"Sorry, are you?" Harriet snapped in a papery voice that sounded so different from the warm, maternal tones he remembered. "Then take me home. They steal things here. My wedding ring—"

Terri took one bony hand and lifted it to the light. "Look, Grandma. Your ring is right here on your finger. Nobody stole it."

"Liar! That old thing isn't my ring!" The old woman snatched her hand away. "Where's Steve? He never lied to me! I want him to come and take me home!"

Still standing in the doorway, Buck felt the painful tightening in his gut. It hurt for him to watch this. But how much worse would it be for Terri, dealing with this poor woman every day?

And why couldn't Steve have been here? Why had Steve been the one to die, when it should have been him?

"Look, Grandma." Terri drew her attention toward the doorway. "You've got visitors."

"Oh?" Harriet perked up. "Who is it? Is it Steve?"

"No, it's Steve's friend Buck. And he brought his little girl. Her name's Quinn." She beckoned them over.

Quinn gripped her father's hand. Maybe Terri had been right about this experience being too much for her. But it was too late to back out now.

"Hello, Mrs. Cooper." He offered her his free hand.

Her dim eyes brightened. "Steve! It's really you! Did you come to take me home?"

Buck steeled his emotions. "I'm Buck, Mrs. Cooper. I used to come to your house with Steve."

Her grip on his hand was surprisingly strong. "You were always my favorite, Steve. More than your sister. Why'd you stay away such a long time?"

He cast a helpless glance at Terri. She was doing her best to remain smiling and composed. "This is Buck, Grandma," she said. "And here's his little girl."

"Steve's little girl." She reached out and touched Quinn's cheek. "My, but you're a pretty thing. Come give your great-grandma a kiss."

Buck could feel Quinn trembling next to him. But she stepped forward and feathered a kiss on the wrinkled cheek. Buck had never been more proud of his daughter.

The old woman fixed her cataract-blurred gaze on him. "So, why are you just standing there? Get me up and take me home."

"Grandma—" Terri began, but she was interrupted by a polite tap on the already-open door. The aides, thank heaven, had arrived to get Harriet ready for bed.

"No—I'm going home!" the old woman protested as one of the young women started unbuttoning her sweater.

"It'll be all right, Grandma. I'll see you tomorrow. We'll talk then." Terri kissed her grandmother, and the three of them made their exit down the hallway to the elevator.

"I'm sorry about the mix-up," Terri said as they walked out the front door. "She does have good days... but I'm afraid the bad ones have become a lot more common. Lately, every time I come here, she breaks my heart."

"But at least you keep coming. I've got to hand it to you, Terri. I had no idea she was so bad. Is there anything I can do to help?"

Terri shook her head. "All she wants is to go home. One of these days she will."

Quinn, usually so chatty, had fallen silent. Buck hoped he could get her to talk on the way home. She needed to process what she'd seen and heard. But meanwhile, he needed to stall Terri a little longer so she wouldn't interrupt the first part of his campaign to show her how valuable she was to him.

"Hey, how about ice cream sundaes?" he said. "The best ice cream parlor in town is right across the street!"

Quinn brightened. "Sounds yummy!"

"I really need to get back to my Jeep," Terri said, moving on. "You two go ahead and get your sundaes. It's a nice evening, and I could use the exercise of the walk back."

"Oh, come on." Buck caught her arm, his grip hard enough to stop her in her tracks. "Quinn's here. Doesn't that call for a party? We can drop you off when we're finished."

She sighed. "Okay. Ice cream does sound good."

They entered the ice cream parlor, ordered hot fudge sundaes at the counter and found a booth. The place was done in pink-and-black '50s decor with vintage rock and roll playing in the background. An elderly couple was holding hands at a corner table. The man was laughing, the woman tapping her toe to the beat. Quinn watched them a moment before she spoke.

"Do I have a grandma?" She showered her sundae with sprinkles from a canister on the table.

"Your mother's mother lives in Florida," Buck said. "She's your grandma."

"She doesn't count. She and Mom are mad at each other. They don't even send each other Christmas cards. What about your mother? How come I don't know her?"

Buck had known that sooner or later she was bound to ask. But he'd never looked forward to answering. "She died when I was in the army, before I married your mother. She had lung cancer—from smoking."

"What about your dad? He'd be my grandpa."

"I never knew him. He went away before I was born."

"And he never came back?"

"He never did. My mother raised me on her own. She was a waitress at the old truck stop out by the main highway. We were so poor we lived on the left-over food she brought home." Buck didn't tell her his parents had never married, or that his mother had done more than wait tables at that truck stop. Some truths were better kept in silence.

"If you were so poor, how did you get rich, Daddy?"

"Smart thinking, lots of hard work—and good help-ers like Terri."

"Is Terri rich, too?"

Buck glanced across the table at Terri. She was nibbling her sundae, avoiding his gaze. He paid her a good salary, but after what he'd seen tonight, he was pretty sure she spent most of her money on her grand-mother's care. When she didn't answer Quinn's ques-tion, he answered for her. "Terri's not nearly as rich as she deserves to be."

Guilt chewed at him, drawing blood. The old woman was Steve's grandmother, too. If Steve had lived, Terri wouldn't have had to shoulder the burden of her care alone. Nursing homes weren't cheap, but for Buck the money would be pocket change. He'd call Canyon Shadows tomorrow and make some arrangements. Or maybe he ought to just buy the place. It was decently maintained and would likely be a good investment.

But what was he thinking? After a day like today, he was in no frame of mind for business decisions.

His gaze wandered back to Terri. She looked irresistible, with tendrils of windblown hair framing her face and a little smear of chocolate fudge on her upper lip. If they'd been alone he'd have been tempted to lean over and lick it off. He'd never had thoughts like this about her before—had always viewed her strictly as a friend. But now that he knew how good it could be between them...

The memory slammed him—Terri leaning over him, straddling his hips as he thrust deep. And this time he could visualize her face, eyes closed, lips sensually parted.

Damn!

The lady was off-limits for so many reasons. And she was driving him crazy.

After the ice cream sundaes, Terri had finally managed to convince Buck that she wanted to walk back to her Jeep. The distance wasn't far—only about seven blocks—and she truly needed to clear her head. As the Hummer drove away, she blew a last kiss to Quinn and set out.

By now it was nearly dark, but Main Street was

still busy, the shops and cafés doing a bustling business. The tiny white lights that adorned the sycamores along the boardwalk had come on, their glitter creating a festive atmosphere. But Terri's mood was far from festive. From beginning to end, this had been the most emotional day in recent memory.

Quinn's presence tonight had been a godsend. She had no idea what she'd have said to Buck, or what he might have said to her, if they'd found themselves alone together. From his flirting with the waitress at dinner, it was clear that he wasn't interested in pursuing anything with Terri. She'd been foolish to even consider the possibility. Maybe she should just forget it had ever happened. Expect nothing—that was the only way to survive life with Buck.

Her thoughts shifted to their visit with her grandmother. Had it upset Buck to be mistaken for Steve? The two had been like brothers all their lives. Buck had been there in Iraq with their combat unit when Steve died. He'd never talked about it, and she'd never asked him, but Terri knew her brother's death had affected him as deeply as it had her.

She could understand why he'd insisted on ice cream tonight. He'd wanted to blur the memory and end the evening on a happy note. But the conversation with Quinn had only opened more dark windows on the past.

Terri knew about Buck's troubled childhood. And she knew how far his mother, a desperate but kind-hearted woman, had gone to provide for her boy. Terri could only hope he had forgiven her.

Terri's long legs covered the seven blocks back to Giovanni's at a brisk pace. Through the deepening twilight, she could make out her Jeep at the far end of the parking lot. She felt for the keys, pulled them out of her purse and strode toward the vehicle.

Had Buck's crew fixed her flat tire, or would she have to haul out the jack and the lug wrench and do it herself? No big deal—she'd changed tires before. And at least that way, she wouldn't feel beholden to Buck. After this morning, she never wanted to feel obligated to him again. To use the old-fashioned expression, it would be too much like being paid for her favors.

She was a few yards away from the Jeep when the parking lot's overhead lights flashed on. In the sudden glare Terri saw what the shadows had hidden.

The flat tire hadn't just been changed. It had been replaced, along with the other three. Her ancient Jeep was now sporting four brand-new, top-of-the-line tires.

Terri stared at Buck's gift. What had the man been thinking? He could certainly afford to replace her tires. But why had he done it, especially without asking her? Did he think he owed her some kind of reward for her...*services*? Or had he done it out of some twisted sense of guilt for taking her to bed in the first place?

Either way, she wasn't going to let this stand.

"Daddy, why did Terri's grandma call you Steve?" Quinn had been silent most of the way home. When she finally spoke, her question, coming out of the cab's darkness, caught Buck off guard.

"She's old," he said. "She can't see very well, and sometimes her thoughts get confused. It's sad, but it happens to some old people. That's why she's at Canyon Shadows, so the nurses can take care of her."

"But who's Steve?" Quinn persisted. "Is somebody who looks like you?"

Buck tapped the brake as a mule deer bounded through the headlights and vanished into the brush on the far side of the road.

"Steve was Terri's brother and my best friend. He died in the war. It was a long time ago, before you were born. But his grandmother doesn't remember that."

"How did he die?"

"He was a soldier. He got shot." Buck struggled to block the images that flashed through his mind. He wished his daughter would talk about something else.

"That's sad." Quinn's profile was a dark silhouette against the side window. "Where did they bury him?"

"Right here in Porter Hollow. His grave is in the cemetery." Buck pressed the remote button to open the wrought iron gate to his property. "What would you like to do tomorrow, besides clothes shopping with Terri?"

"I want to go to the cemetery."

"What on earth for?" Buck bit back a curse as he gunned the Hummer up the steep driveway to the house. He knew Quinn was curious. But there was nothing in the cemetery he cared to show her, let alone see again himself.

"I've never been to a cemetery. I want to see what it's like. I want to see your mother's grave—she'd be my grandma if she was alive. And I want to see where Steve is buried."

"Maybe Terri can take you after you go shopping." It was the coward's way out to dump this on Terri, but Buck really couldn't go himself. He had some wealthy clients from Dubai coming in this afternoon to raft the Grand Canyon. He wanted to greet them personally and make sure everything was up to their standard of luxury. He'd been weighing the idea of building a second resort in the southeast corner of the state, near Moab, with access to Arches and Monument Valley. So far it was just a dream, but if he decided to go ahead, a hefty infusion of Dubai cash could make it happen sooner.

If nothing else came of it, at least he'd have an excuse not to visit the cemetery and relive the past with Quinn.

"What else would you like to do?" he asked his daughter. "I can have Terri line up anything you'd like. Oh, and I've asked Mrs. Calloway to be on hand while you're here. She can take you if you want to go somewhere."

"Daddy, I'm nine years old!" Quinn stormed. "I'm not a baby, and I don't need a babysitter."

"Well, you do need to eat, and Mrs. Calloway's a good cook."

"That still doesn't mean I have to be babysat. Mrs. Calloway won't let me out of her sight. She's a nice lady, but she drives me crazy. She even sits right by the pool when I'm in the water. Last year I asked her if she could swim. She shook her head. If she had to rescue me, she'd probably drown."

"Mrs. Calloway is just doing her job," Buck said. "The agreement I have with your mother says that while you're here you have to be supervised."

"Why can't I just hang out with Terri?"

Buck ignored the slight jolt triggered by the mention of Terri's name. He wondered what she'd thought when she'd discovered the new tires on her Jeep. He'd done it in the spirit of helping her out, but would she see it that way? Maybe he should have left well enough alone.

"Terri has to work," he said. "I need her help in the office."

"Then why can't I hang out with you?" Quinn asked. "You're the boss. Nobody tells you when you have to work."

"The boss has to work the hardest of all. That's why he's the boss. I'll be busy all day tomorrow. But Terri will pick you up in the afternoon. You'll be fine."

"Sure." Quinn sighed like a deflating balloon and slumped in the seat. She was silent till the Hummer pulled into the driveway and stopped. Buck had barely switched off the engine when she opened the door, piled out of the vehicle and ran to the fence, where

Murphy was waiting to welcome her with barks and whimpers of joy.

"Hi, Murphy!" She reached her small hands through the chain links to pet the huge dog, whose wagging tail could have felled a forest of small trees. "How've you been, boy? Hey, I can hang out with you, can't I? At least *somebody's* got time for me!"

Giving Buck a meaningful scowl, she stalked onto the porch and waited for her father to unlock the front door.

The next morning Terri came in early, opened the door to Buck's private office and left something on his desk. He wouldn't be happy when he found it, but she was braced for the storm. If the boss man didn't like it, he could fire her.

Minutes later, she was at her own desk, answering emails, when Buck walked in. His office had its own outside entrance, but today he came in from the hotel lobby side. Standing in the open doorway of her office, he gave her a casual smile and extended a closed fist. "Here. Hold out your hand."

Terri reached across the desk. Opening his fist, he dropped something into her palm. Even before she looked at it, she knew it was her missing earring.

Terri willed her expression to freeze into a calm mask. Did this mean he was going to tell her how he came to find it? Her pulse kicked into overdrive. After ten years, was their relationship finally about to move out of its familiar rut?

She waited for him to close her office door for more

privacy. Instead he remained where he was, the same disarming smile on his face.

"The grounds crew found your earring in the parking lot," he said. "It's a lucky thing it didn't get run over."

Terri felt the sudden catch of her breath, as if she'd just been gut-punched. Instead of owning up to what had happened between them, he'd chosen to lie. The unfeeling jerk hadn't even cared enough to be honest.

It was time she faced reality. Aside from her general usefulness, Buck didn't care about her at all—and if sleeping with him hadn't changed anything, nothing ever would.

"Thanks," she said, wrapping the earring in a tissue and sliding it into her purse. "The other one's at home. It'll be nice to have the pair again."

He remained a moment, framed by the doorway. Was he waiting for some kind of confession from her? Well, the man would grow a long gray beard before he'd get one.

The standoff was broken by the first phone call of the day. As Terri took the call, from a possible client, Buck turned away and walked back toward his office.

Terri took her time on the phone, answering questions and jotting down information. Out in the common room, the summer temps were arriving, chatting on the way to their desks. Terri hung up the phone and waited. By now, Buck would have found the check she'd written and left in an envelope on his desk. Waiting for his reaction was like waiting for the fall of an ax. But this confrontation had to happen. Her pride demanded it—especially in view of the lie he'd just told her.

It was a matter of seconds before he reappeared in her doorway. His eyes were steely, his jaw set in a grim line. "In my office, Terri," he demanded. "Now."

Four

Terri walked ahead of Buck, feeling like an errant schoolgirl being herded into the principal's office. Curious gazes followed them. Buck hadn't said another word, but his stride and his stormy expression gave off signals that somebody was in trouble.

As the door closed behind them, he turned toward his desk, picked up the check that lay next to the phone and waved it in her face. "What is this, Terri?" he demanded.

She raised her chin. "It's just what it looks like. I'm paying you back for the tires you put on my Jeep. Let me know if it isn't enough."

Terri had looked up the price of the tires online. They were top quality, almost sixteen hundred dollars for the set. Covering the payment had all but cleaned out her checking account, but she had her pride, and she wasn't about to back down.

Buck's scowl darkened. "I wanted to *give* you those tires. You needed and deserved them."

Deserved them? How? Oh—did I do something special for you?

Terri had to bite back the sarcastic retort. The fact that they'd had sex the day before was the proverbial elephant in the room. But if he wasn't going to acknowledge it, then neither was she. She'd been an impulsive fool, letting her boss pull her into bed and foolishly thinking it might actually change things between them. Right now all she wanted was to forget it had ever happened.

"I don't want your money, Terri. If you want to repay me, just take the check, say thank you and go back to work."

Terri lifted her chin higher, fixing him with a narrow-eyed gaze. "I'm your employee, not your charity case, Buck. I'm not taking that check back. If it doesn't clear the bank in the next three days, you're going to find four tires piled on your front porch. I can get perfectly decent tires for a lot less than these cost—in fact, I was planning to just that."

"Fine. You win," he snapped. "I'll cash the damned check. Just remember to drop by the vehicle department and get your wheels balanced and aligned. My crew couldn't do that in the parking lot. And no, you don't have to pay them."

Terri could feel the emotions welling—anger, embarrassment and frustration. Her throat choked off. Her eyes stung with unshed tears. "I'll take care of my own wheels, thank you," she said. "I won't be using the services of your vehicle department because..." The words were on the tip of her tongue, but she wasn't sure she could say them.

She felt light-headed. Had she gone too far? No, she had to do this. It was time.

"Because why?" he asked.

"Because I'm quitting, Buck. I'm giving you my two weeks' notice, starting right now."

Buck stared after her as she stalked out and closed the door. She hadn't meant it, of course. She was riled, that was all. Give her a little time to cool down, and she'd be fine.

I'm quitting, Buck. I'm giving you my two weeks' notice, starting right now.

Her words echoed like the memory of a bad dream. There was no way Terri could quit now, or even in two weeks—not when he needed her so much. Summer was the busy season here, with important clients coming in, and the big charity gala less than a month off. And what would he do about Quinn? She'd be devastated if Terri left.

Lord, what if she'd meant it? What if she was really going to quit?

She could do it, Buck realized. He knew of a half dozen places that would hire her in a minute. And she wouldn't have that much trouble selling her grand-

mother's property or relocating Harriet to a new facility. In two weeks she could have everything settled
and be ready to move out of his life.

No way was he going to let that happen. He had to
come up with some kind of plan. But that was easier
said than done.

First off, it would help him to know why she'd been
so upset. Was it because he'd bought her tires or because of what had happened in his bed? He could try
talking to her about it—but he'd resolved not to show
that he remembered their morning romp. Telling her
the truth would only add to the complications.

Terri's check for sixteen hundred dollars lay on his
desk. He would cash it as promised, then apply the
money, and more, to her grandmother's care at Canyon
Shadows. Terri might not like him paying for something else behind her back, but with luck she wouldn't
find out anytime soon. She was independent to a fault.
But he'd promised Steve he'd take care of her. Besides,
he'd discovered that he liked the way taking care of
Terri made him feel.

Last night, when he'd arranged to replace her tires,
he'd weighed the idea of surprising her with a brand-
new vehicle. But that old Jeep had been Steve's. There
was no way Terri would part with it. She would drive
it till it rusted away to a pile of nuts and bolts.

Still, it didn't make sense that doing Terri a favor
would push her to quit her job. There had to be more
behind her reasons. Whatever was driving her away

from him, he couldn't afford to lose her. He had to find a way to make her stay.

Forcing the thought aside for now, he turned on his computer and brought up his agenda for the day—the agenda Terri, as always, had prepared the day before. This morning Evie would be taking the jet, along with a flight steward, to meet the Dubai clients at the airport in Salt Lake City. The four oil-rich sheikhs would expect nothing but the best—gourmet snacks on the flight south, then a private lunch in the restaurant's dining room. Buck would be meeting the plane at the company airstrip, hosting the lunch, and taking them on a helicopter tour of Zion and Canyonlands National Parks, to be followed by an outdoor barbecue and a night's rest. Tomorrow morning, after breakfast, a helicopter would fly them to Lee's Ferry to board the raft for their three-day trip down the Colorado River, to Phantom Ranch in the canyon bottom. From there they would ride mules up the trail to the South Rim, where they could spend a night in the lodge. The next morning, Evie would fly them to Las Vegas in the jet.

Everything had been planned down to the last detail—the best guide and boat pilot available, the best food, and two camp boys who could cook and entertain as well as set up the tents and the portable latrine. He needed everything to be perfect, because if the sheikhs enjoyed the trip, they might take an interest in backing his new project.

Buck hadn't planned to go along on the river excursion. He had other things to do. And he had complete

faith in the people he was sending. There was no reason not to expect a successful trip. But he'd made his
plans before Terri's announcement that she was quitting. Now a sudden idea struck him.

Three days in the beautiful canyon, away from
ringing phones and interruptions, might be just the
ticket for talking Terri into staying around. He knew
she loved this place—he just had to remind her. He'd
have no trouble juggling his schedule to include himself in the trip. The challenge would be getting Terri
to go along.

If he asked her, she was bound to make excuses,
or even refuse to go. Rather than risk that, he would
need to figure out a way to shanghai her.

Buck had hoped to free up some time for Quinn.
But that would have to wait. The prospect of losing
Terri was a five-alarm emergency.

After a busy morning, Terri phoned to tell Quinn
she was coming to pick her up. "Is there any special
place you'd like to look for clothes?" she asked.

"Anyplace away from here!" Quinn sighed. "Mrs.
C. is driving me crazy. She follows me around like
she's the Secret Service."

"Well, I'm betting she could use a break, too," Terri
said. "I'll see you in about twenty minutes."

Terri switched off her computer and stuck a note
to the screen. She planned to come back at the end
of the day to post the agenda and clean up any loose
ends Bob and the temps might have left. With Buck

off entertaining the Dubai clients, somebody needed to make sure everything was shipshape for tomorrow's river launch.

Quinn was waiting on the porch when Terri pulled up to the house. Like an escaping prisoner, she raced down the steps and clambered into the Jeep. "Let's go!" she said.

"Hold your horses, girl." Terri waited while the plump, middle-aged widow, dressed in a blue seersucker pantsuit, came out onto the porch. "I'll have her back here by four, Mrs. Calloway. Meanwhile, relax and enjoy some peace and quiet."

Quinn giggled as the Jeep pulled out of the driveway. "Maybe she'll take a bubble bath in Dad's Jacuzzi. God knows she needs to do something to loosen up."

"Stop that, Quinn," Terri chided the girl. "Mrs. Calloway's just doing her job. You know the woman would fight off man-eating tigers to keep you safe."

"At least it would be fun to see her do that," Quinn said. "Where are you taking me?"

"To the outlet mall at the junction. No sense spending a lot of money on clothes you'll just grow out of. Okay?"

"Sure. I just need jeans and shorts and shirts—and a jacket and a new swimsuit. Oh, and new underwear. Hey, can I get a bra?"

"You're nine." Terri glanced at the girl's flat chest. "Aren't you a little young for a bra?"

"A girl in my class has one. She showed it to me. She thinks she's *so* hot."

"I think the bra can wait till you're older." Terri swung the Jeep onto the highway. The outlet mall was ten miles down the road, a shopping mecca for the surrounding towns and farms.

"Can we get burgers and fries and shakes? Mrs. C. only feeds me healthy, balanced meals."

Terri suppressed a smile. "Okay. After we're done shopping."

Buying the clothes Quinn needed took a little less than two hours. By the time they'd finished their burgers, it was after three o'clock. "We need to get you home," Terri said as they climbed into the Jeep. "I promised to have you back by four, and I don't want Mrs. Calloway to worry."

"Daddy said you'd take me to the cemetery. I want to see where my grandma's buried."

Terri hesitated, thinking of the time. "All right. It's on the way back to town. We can stop there, but we'll only have a few minutes."

"That'll be enough," Quinn said.

"Okay. Let's go. Fasten your seat belt."

The cemetery was small and old, many of the weathered markers dating back to pioneer times. Hundred-year-old pine trees sheltered the graves. Spring grass covered the ground in patches. Among the headstones, the delicate hoofprints of mule deer etched tracery-like paths in the russet earth.

Terri knew where Buck's mother was buried.

Quinn's hand crept into hers as they stood beside the grave and read the inscription on the small, plain marble slab.

Annie Morgan
July 10, 1953–August 14, 2001

"How old was she when she died?" Quinn asked.

"Not old at all, not even fifty," Terri said, thinking even that number would sound old to someone as young as Quinn.

"Was she nice?"

"She was always nice," Terri said, holding back the words *Too nice for her own good*, remembering the stories about the truck stop. Annie Morgan had been small and sad and had seemed desperately lonely— and sometimes just plain desperate—but she'd always been kind to Terri and Steve. "If she was still alive I think she'd be a good grandma to you."

"I wish I'd brought a flower or something," Quinn said.

"You can always come back."

Quinn's gaze followed the flight of a dragonfly. "Where's Steve's grave?" she asked.

"How did you know Steve was buried here?" Terri asked, mildly surprised.

"Daddy told me. He said Steve was your brother and his best friend, but that he died in the war."

"It's in the next row. I'll show you." Together they walked to the bronze plaque, set in concrete and flanked by a metal bracket where a flag could be placed on Memorial Day.

"Did he have a girlfriend?"

"He did. But after he died she married somebody else and moved away." Terri glanced at her watch. They had a few more minutes to spare. "This next grave is my grandfather's. He passed away before I was born. And this empty spot next to him is where my grandma will be buried."

Quinn had fallen silent. This talk of death was a lot for a nine-year-old to wrap her mind around. She'd likely had enough.

"Time to go." Terri led the way back to the Jeep. Twenty minutes later they pulled up to the house. Mrs. Calloway, looking relieved, was waiting on the porch.

Quinn unfastened her seat belt and leaned over the gearshift to give Terri a hug. "This was the best time ever," she said. "Can you come back again tomorrow?"

Terri hugged her back. "We'll see. That depends on what your dad needs me to do. I'll call you, okay?"

"Okay." Quinn grabbed her shopping bags and climbed out of the Jeep. With a farewell wave, Terri backed down the driveway and through the gate. There was work still waiting for her at the office.

Quinn had had such a good time today, she mused. It didn't take much to make the little girl happy, just somebody to be with her and pay attention to her— preferably without smothering her, the way Mrs. Calloway did. Maybe it would help to talk with Buck and let him know how much his daughter needed him.

A shadow darkened her thoughts as she remembered giving him her notice that morning. She was determined to go through with her plans. But leaving Quinn when the girl had so few people she could rely on would break her heart. Maybe in the time she had left, she could work on getting Buck to spend more time with his daughter—or at least help Quinn find some friends.

By the time she returned to the office, the staff was gone. The ceiling lights had been turned off, casting the common room into late-afternoon shadows. Terri was walking toward her office when she noticed Buck's door was ajar.

In her absence, it had been Bob's responsibility to make sure the place was securely locked. Evidently the young man's thoughts had been elsewhere—one more thing she would have to remind him about tomorrow.

She'd reached Buck's door and was about to lock it when she realized the room wasn't empty. Buck was sitting in the shadows, his chair turned toward the window. Terri understood him well enough to know that he was troubled. Was he upset about her quitting, or had something else gone wrong?

"Are you all right?" Terri asked softly.

"Oh, it's you." With a bitter chuckle, he swiveled the chair toward her. "How did things go with Quinn today?"

"Fine. We had a good time. But what are you doing here?"

Buck shook his head. "Sit down, Terri. I hope you're in a patient mood because I need a good listener."

"What is it?" Terri took the chair on the near side of Buck's desk. "Did everything go all right with the sheikhs?"

"Like clockwork." He paused, taking a deep breath. "Evie was there to pick them up on time, smooth flight and park tour, first-rate lunch…" His voice trailed off. "Terri, would you ever call me naive?"

She met his troubled gaze. "Why?" she asked. "What happened?"

"This would make a funny story if it wasn't so frustrating. Everything went swimmingly with the sheikhs. By the time we'd finished the tour and come back to the hotel, I was congratulating myself on money and effort well spent. Then it came time for me to see them to their rooms for a rest before the barbecue…" He gave a bitter chuckle. "I realized they were looking at me, as if expecting more. Finally the tallest one, who did most of the talking, took me aside and asked me—" Buck broke off, shaking his head.

"What?"

"He asked me, 'Where are the girls?'"

Terri's jaw dropped as the implication sank home. "Oh, Buck!"

"I should've expected this," he said. "I should have realized what they'd expect and made it clear before they even came that none of that would be happening here. I wear a lot of hats in this business, but the one thing I'm not, and won't ever be, is a damned pimp."

"So what did you tell them?"

"What could I tell them? I said that girls weren't part of the package. They were polite enough, even when I turned down the extra money they offered me, but I could tell they weren't happy about it. And something tells me they won't be offering to back my new resort."

"I'm so sorry." Terri knew how much planning and effort had gone into this venture. Buck's disappointment was evident in his tired voice and every line of his face. Terri checked the urge to move behind his chair and rub his shoulders. Two days ago she might have done it. But not now.

"What about the river trip?" she asked. "Is it still on for tomorrow?"

"Yes, they still want to go. Which reminds me, Terri, we've got a couple of the staff out sick. The equipment truck's loaded and ready to go, but I'll need you to drive it down to Lee's Ferry and bring it back here once the gear's unloaded.

Terri stifled a groan. She knew what that meant. She'd be leaving at 4:00 a.m. with the two camp boys, to be at the landing with the big trailer truck, which held the two uninflated rafts, the air pump, the food and cooking supplies, the tents, the portable latrine and the other gear. By the time the clients arrived by helicopter at eight thirty the rafts would be inflated, loaded and ready to go—one for the clients and the other for the gear. After that, she'd make the two-hour solo drive back to the resort.

"Sorry to dump this on you at the last minute," Buck said, as if reading her thoughts. "I'd drive the truck myself, but I'll be helicoptering in with the sheikhs. I've decided to guide the river trip myself. Maybe I can still salvage the situation."

Terri counted the hours the round-trip in the truck would take out of her day. Not good timing. She had a lot to do tomorrow, and she'd wanted to spend more time with Quinn—even more so now that Buck had said he'd be going on the trip with the sheikhs. With her father gone, the girl would be lonesome. "Isn't there anybody else who can haul the gear down?" she asked. "Bob, maybe?"

"He's not licensed to drive that big truck. If he has a problem, the insurance company won't pay."

"Fine." Terri sighed and shrugged. "I've done it before. No reason I can't do it again."

"Thanks. And just one more thing, Terri."

Her pulse quickened. Maybe this was the moment. Maybe he was going to ask her to stay—and not just for the job, but for *him*.

"I know you've given your two weeks' notice," he said. "But I'm hoping I can talk you into staying through the gala. It's only another week or so—and it'll be a mess without you. I'll pay you a bonus, of course. Name your price."

She should have known better. Feeling as if she'd

just been slapped with a frozen fish, Terri rose from her chair. "I'll let you know after you're back from the river run. But you'll have to make it worth my time." She walked to the door, then turned. "If you don't mind a suggestion, why don't you go home and spend some quality time with your daughter before tomorrow?"

"Good idea, but I need to check the supplies for the trip and make sure everything's on the truck. By then it'll be time for the barbecue with the sheikhs. You're welcome to come if you like."

"Not on your life. They're all yours."

"See you tomorrow, then." Rising, he moved to the outside door of his office and opened it. "Thanks again for agreeing to drive the truck. I appreciate your help."

"It's my job." Her voice dripped icicles, but Buck didn't seem to notice.

He left and closed the door. Terri double-checked to make sure both doors to his office were locked, then returned to her own office and switched on her computer. The sooner she got today's work done, the sooner she could go home and rest up for an early start tomorrow. She wasn't happy about driving the truck, and even less happy about the way he'd taken her for granted yet again. She should have walked out on the spot and left him with his movie-star mouth hanging open.

Buck didn't care about her as a woman. He never had and he never would. She'd consider staying through the gala as he'd asked because she knew how much it meant to the business and she didn't want to let anyone down, but once that was over, she'd leave this place—and that man—behind for good.

The heavy trailer truck rumbled over the narrow road, swaying dangerously every time a wheel sank into a pothole. Half-blinded by the sunrise above the red-rock mesas, Terri ground the gears and wrestled with the wheel. Years ago, at Buck's suggestion, she'd learned the skills, and acquired the paperwork, to fill in for almost any job in the company. Not only could she drive the truck, she was licensed as a skydive instructor, bungee-jumping instructor and boat pilot. She was also a fair mechanic and certified in first aid and lifesaving. When Buck referred to her as his right-hand woman he wasn't just throwing out words. Anything he could do, she could do almost as well, if not better. It was a situation that backfired on her often when, like today, she was the only person on hand qualified to do an unpleasant task.

Next to her on the single bench seat, the two camp boys were catching some extra sleep. Still in their early twenties, they were both seasoned river runners. It would be their job to motor ahead in the loaded supply raft, set up camp and have everything ready when the clients arrived at the end of the day's run. At Phantom Ranch, where the adventure would end, they would put a tow on the client raft and continue all the way to Lake Mead, where both rafts would be hauled out of the water, unloaded, deflated and trucked home.

Eli Rasmussen, a local boy with freckles and red hair, was snoring, his mouth open, his head drooping to one side. George Redfeather, Evie's nephew, handsome and polite, had fallen into a quiet doze. Glancing at them, Terri smiled. Both young men were good-humored and likable. Eli could sing and play the guitar, and George was a master Native American storyteller. They'd been Buck's first choice for this trip, and she knew they would give it their all. For their sakes, Terri could only hope the four sheikhs would be generous tippers.

Up ahead, she could make out the low prefab buildings that marked Lee's Ferry, the launching point for boats running down Marble Canyon, into the Colorado River and through the Grand Canyon. She checked her watch. Time to wake the boys. With her help, they'd have a little over an hour to get everything ready before the helicopter was due.

One vital member of the team would be meeting them here. Arnie Bowles, an expert river pilot, lived in Page, the big town near the Glen Canyon Dam. He'd be dropped off by his wife, Peggy. Terri glanced around for him as she pulled the truck into the parking lot. He was nowhere to be seen.

"Maybe Arnie had car trouble." Eli had jumped out of the cab and was opening the back of the trailer.

"Maybe so. He usually gets here early." Terri began moving the food coolers out of the way while George hauled the first of two outboard motors down to the water's edge. They worked swiftly and efficiently, each one knowing exactly what needed to be done.

Half an hour later, Arnie had yet to arrive. Terri was getting concerned. He had her cell number, as did the office, but no one had called her. Maybe Buck had heard something.

At eight thirty, they heard the whirr of the approaching helicopter. Minutes later, the machine touched down, sending up clouds of red dust before the rotors slowed. Buck jumped to the ground. The four sheikhs, swarthy, handsome men dressed in rain gear for the river, climbed out behind him.

Spotting Terri, Buck beckoned her close. "There's been a change of plans," he said. "Arnie can't make it. We'll need you to take his place."

Terri's eyes went wide. "But—"

"Listen to me." His gaze drilled into her. "If you can't do the job, we'll have to cancel the whole trip."

"You can't reschedule for tomorrow?"

"No time. They're due for meetings in Vegas right after the trip." He leaned close to her. "Listen, Terri, they're already disappointed about the girls. The only way to salvage this is to give them a good river run."

"But what about the office? What about Quinn— and my grandmother?"

"It's only for three days. We can cover that. I'll make some calls."

Before Terri could protest again, he turned back to

the four men. "We're good," he said. "Give us a few minutes, and we'll push off."

Terri knew better than to argue. Once Buck made up his mind there was no stopping him.

She had just a few more weeks to put up with his high-handed insensitivity. After that, Buck Morgan, the ten years she'd been at his side and that one hot encounter in his bed would be history.

Thankfully, Arnie's rain gear, needed for protection against the chilling spray of the river, had been stowed in the client boat. While Buck made his calls, she decided to get the waterproof pants and jacket, and slip the set over her clothes. But first, knowing what could happen to possessions on the river, she gave her purse to the helicopter pilot, a man she trusted, and asked him to leave it at the hotel desk for her.

To get to the waiting rafts, she had to walk between the truck and the clients, who were standing in a close group. As she passed the tallest of the four men, she felt an unexpected press on the seat of her khakis.

Terri stifled a gasp. There could be no mistaking that touch. That arrogant, billionaire jerk had just patted her on the rump.

Five

The river was swollen with spring runoff, its water chocolate brown with silt. Calm, rippling stretches alternated with wild rapids that raced and tumbled, spraying the air with mist.

Terri knew the river like the back of her hand. She used the outboard motor to steer the raft into the spots that would make for an exhilarating but safe run, letting the rapids carry it downstream. The four sheikhs whooped and cheered as the flat-bottomed rubber raft bounced and slithered over the roiling water, roaring with laughter as the cold, muddy spray drenched them from head to toe.

Buck had introduced them by name—Abdul, Omar, Hassan and one more she'd already forgotten. Matching those names with faces was more than her busy mind could handle, especially when she was running on a mix of aggravation and insufficient sleep. To keep them straight in her head, she'd renamed them Eeny, Meeny, Miney and Moe—in order of their height.

Eeny was the one to watch.

Scanning the river ahead, she steered right to avoid a jutting rock. This was the easy part of her job. She could simply pilot the raft, ignored by the clients as they enjoyed the ride, and by Buck who sat in front, pointing out interesting sights and lecturing on the geologic history of the canyon. For now she could relax. But that pat on her rear had put her on high alert. Once they reached camp she would have to watch her back. She mustn't let herself be caught alone or give any hint that she might be available. Having to slap a client's face would be bad for Buck's business.

They'd be camping in the canyon three nights, then riding mules up the long, steep trail to the South Rim. She could handle the physical rigors of the journey, but between the discomfort of being the only woman and her worry about the duties she'd left behind, Terri was already anxious for the trip to end.

Buck hadn't even given her a chance to back out. As always he'd ignored her needs and taken for granted that she'd do what he wanted.

All the more reason to quit and move on.

Buck's eyes swept the sheer sandstone cliffs that rose on both sides of the river. Then his gaze shifted to the rear of the raft, where Terri sat with one hand on the tiller. Even in the oversize rain gear she wore, she looked every inch a woman. He'd seen the way the four men looked at her, especially Abdul, and he didn't like it. In their culture, an unveiled female, especially a pretty one, might easily be seen as fair game, especially since they were already paying for her services as river pilot.

He could hardly put her in a burka. But once they got to camp he would need to keep her in sight and make it clear to the men that female employees were off-limits.

Off-limits.

This trip was supposed to make Terri fall in love with the area again and choose to stay. The last thing he wanted was for her to get so fed up with ogling clients that she'd be even more determined to leave.

Besides, Abdul had no right to think of Terri as someone he was entitled to due to his money and position. Terri deserved more respect than that—and she knew it. They'd had plenty of rich men and celebrities in and out of the resort through the years, and Terri had never been dazzled or overawed by anyone. She wasn't the type to fall into a stranger's bed just because she was flattered by his attention or impressed by his wealth.

His thoughts spiraled back to that interlude in his bedroom, with Terri leaning above him, eyes closed, moist lips parted, hair hanging down to brush his face as she moved above him, pushing him deep, and deeper, into the honey of her sweet body... Instead of falling into bed with a stranger, she'd fallen into bed with him, and it had been *phenomenal*.

The raft pitched and dived, jarring him back to the present. As they plowed into another stretch of rapids, Buck grabbed the seat to keep from being flung into the water. Best keep his mind on what was happening, he scolded himself. But even then, his gaze was drawn to Terri. With her hood flung back, her wet hair streaming, her eyes bright with excitement, she was so wildly beautiful that she took his breath away.

The realization hit him like a gut punch. He'd had her once and vowed it wouldn't happen again. But right or wrong, he wanted her back—in his arms, in his bed.

Heaven help him, was he falling for his right-hand woman?

With the canyon shadows deepening, the raft crunched onto the broad sand strip below the camp. George was waiting to catch the tether line Buck tossed him and help pull the raft partway out of the water. Terri waited in the stern while the four men climbed out onto dry land—Eeny, Meeny, Miney and Moe. By now she couldn't have remembered their real names for ten thousand dollars. Her body ached from holding herself steady against the pounding current of the river. Her face, hair and rain clothes dripped with muddy water.

The sight of the glowing fire on the high, grassy bank and the aroma of grilling prime rib eye steaks reminded her that she was also hungry. The way the four sheikhs dragged their feet climbing up to the camp gave her hope that they were worn out, too.

Buck had waited for her by the raft. He gave her his hand as she climbed over the inflated bow and jumped to the ground. "Good work, Terri. Thanks for coming along."

"You didn't exactly give me a choice." She was too tired to be gracious.

"Is everything all right? You sound a little ragged around the edges."

"Just unsettled, that's all, and worried about all the things we had to leave hanging. I don't trust Bob's ability to run the office while we're both away. Quinn wanted me to come by. And I didn't even get a chance to check on my grandmother."

"I did ask Bob to call Canyon Shadows and let them know you'd be away."

"Does Quinn know where we are?"

"She was asleep when I got home last night and still asleep when I left this morning. But I spoke with Mrs. Calloway. They'll be fine."

But Quinn won't be happy. You should have at least talked to her. The words hovered on the tip of Terri's tongue, but she bit them back. There was nothing to be done now. They couldn't make phone calls from here. The rafts could communicate with each other by two-way radio. But there was no cell phone service in the canyon. Until they made it up to the South Rim, they'd have better luck calling from the moon.

Supper was eaten around the fire, sitting on camp stools and eating off sturdy paper plates. Eli and George were superb camp cooks—the prime steaks, hot buttered biscuits and roasted corn were all delicious. The three sheikhs Terri had dubbed Meeny, Miney and Moe were polite and pleasant. But Eeny—Abdul, the jerk who'd patted her rump—was already complaining.

"My grandfather lived better than this with his camel herd in the desert. Sleeping on the hard ground in a tent the size of a tabletop, no showers to wash off the mud, no laundry service—and everybody sharing that unspeakable latrine. We at least expected some kind of lodge, with beds and bathrooms."

"This canyon is one of the natural wonders of the world." Buck gazed across the fire, his voice weary but patient as he gave his stock answer. "There are rules we follow to preserve it. The most important rule is that when we leave here, nothing can be left behind. Whatever we bring in has to be brought out—the equipment, the trash, down to the last soda tab. And nothing goes in the river. Even pissing on the bank will get you slapped with a citation." He glanced around the circle of faces. "When you climb off that mule on your fourth day you'll be as tired, sore and filthy as you've ever been in your life. But you'll remember this adventure forever." Like a lawyer resting his case, he rose and walked away from the fire, back toward the tents.

Terri's pulse skittered as the realization struck her.

There were six small dome tents in the camp—one for each of the clients, one to be shared by Eli and George, and another that had been packed for Buck and Arnie. But since Arnie wasn't here, she'd be sharing that one with Buck.

There was nothing to be concerned about, she told herself. They were both exhausted and would probably drop off as soon as they crawled into their sleeping bags. And judging from the glances Abdul was giving her, sharing a tent with Buck would be safer than sleeping alone. The less fuss she made over the situation the better.

Eli had picked up his guitar and was strumming the opening chords of an old Hank Williams song. He had a Hank Williams voice to go with it, and this canyon, with the river whispering and the fire glowing, was the perfect setting for the old-time music. Now, while the men were listening, would be a good time to visit the latrine, Terri thought. Screened by a canvas tarp on poles, the portable device had been set up at the end of a winding path through the willows.

She had finished and was making her way back along the trail, guided by the glow of the campfire beyond the willows, when a dark shape blocked her path.

"Ah, here you are, beautiful one."

Terri's heart sank as she recognized Abdul. She willed herself not to sound nervous. "Yes, I was just on my way back to the fire. The latrine's all yours. Here, I'll step aside so you can get by."

She tried to move out of his way, but his hand

flashed out to clamp her wrist. "I don't have the patience for games," he growled. "A thousand dollars for a night in my tent. If that's not enough you can name your price. I've got the cash. Just wait till the others are asleep, then come to me."

Reining in her anger, Terri willed herself to stay calm and be firm. "No," she said. "I'm not that kind of woman. Just let me go, and we'll forget all about this."

"No, you say?" His grip tightened. "More money, then. Two thousand. Three thousand. Shall I keep going? Any woman can be bought for the right offer. All it takes is enough money to turn her into a whore. Five thousand."

"Let…me…go!" Terri twisted helplessly against the strong hand that clasped her wrist. "Let me go or I'll scream!"

"Let her go, Abdul. Now." Buck's low voice, thin and flat and dangerous, came out of the shadows behind the man. "Do it!" he snarled. "Nobody touches my woman!"

The man dropped his hand, letting her go. "Forgive me, Mr. Morgan. I didn't know she was your property." His tone was edged with mockery. "I should have made the offer to you. Five thousand dollars cash for a night with her."

Buck pushed between Terri and his client. "For five cents, I'd beat you to a bloody pulp and throw you in the river," he snapped. "Go back to the others. Behave yourself, and we'll pretend this never happened. But tell your friends, if you or any of them so much as look at her—"

He let the threat hang, turning to Terri as the man stalked back toward the fire. "Are you all right?" he asked her.

Terri struggled to contain herself. Only now did she realize how scared—and how outraged—she'd been. When she tried to speak, the words emerged between hysterical giggles. "Heavens, what were you thinking, Buck? You could've made yourself five thousand dollars off me!" She dissolved into helpless spasms that bordered on sobs.

"Stop it, Terri." His strong hands gripped her shoulders. As she began to tremble, he pulled her close, holding her hard against his chest. "It's all right, girl. I'm here and, so help me, I won't let that bastard near you."

His clasp calmed her. For a moment Terri let him hold her. She felt safe and protected in his arms—but she knew better than to lower her guard. She was in far more danger with Buck than with the sheikh, because her heart was involved.

She forced a careless laugh. "I'll be fine," she said. "It's a good thing you showed up when you did. Otherwise your billionaire client could've ended up with a bloody nose."

"If he'd hurt you, I'd have given him a lot worse than that." His arms tightened around her. His voice grated with reined anger.

Despite the warning tingle, she tilted her face upward. He leaned close, within a hand's breadth of kissing her. But this time, when the alarm bells went off in her head, she listened. Even if she were fool enough to let him kiss her, this wasn't the time or the place—not when they were facing three nights together in a tiny tent. She pulled away. He let her go.

Still shaken, she tried to make light of the situation. "Wait till I've been on the river a couple more days, with no change of clothes, no makeup, and not even a comb or a toothbrush," she joked, turning back down the path. "I expect my asking price will go way down from five thousand dollars."

He stopped her with a touch on her shoulder. "You don't have to go back to the fire, Terri," he said. "You don't have to face that man again tonight."

"But I do. I need to show him that I'm all right, and that the awful things he said didn't affect me."

"Fine, but I'll come with you," he said, falling into step behind her. "I'm not letting you out of my sight."

"Of course you aren't." She pasted on a mocking smile. "After all, as you said, I'm your woman."

The night was dark, the narrowed sky above the canyon like a river of stars. By lantern light, Buck helped George and Eli stash the last of the dinner gear in the raft, douse the fire and bury the ashes. Breakfast tomorrow would be coffee heated on a propane stove, fresh fruit and pastries, so no morning fire would be needed.

Buck glanced toward Terri. She was huddled on

a flat rock, hugging her knees and looking up at the sky. He knew she must be exhausted—piloting the raft was hard work, and the encounter with Abdul must have left her badly shaken. But even with the four clients zippered into their tents, he didn't want her going to bed until he was ready to go with her. Earlier, he'd taken Eli and George aside and told them what had happened. Now Terri would have three protectors looking out for her.

Terri was one tough lady. She'd be all right, Buck told himself. But he needed her to have a pleasant, relaxing experience on this trip. If she was stressed out from fending off a misbehaving client, his plan to convince her to stay wouldn't stand a chance.

Apart from Abdul, the other sheikhs were all right. They were well mannered and cooperative, and appeared to be enjoying themselves despite the rough conditions. But none of them seemed inclined to stand up to Abdul and correct his behavior. Maybe he outranked them in some way, or maybe they'd known him long enough to accept his conduct.

However, that didn't mean Buck had to put up with it. After the way Abdul had spoken to Terri, the idea of him so much as touching her made Buck want to grab the man by his shirtfront and knock out his front teeth.

Leaving the loaded raft, Buck walked over to where Terri was sitting. "How are you doing?" he asked her.

"Better. The sky makes me feel peaceful. I don't want to punch anybody anymore."

He laughed, enjoying her sense of humor. "Ready to turn in?"

"More than ready. I could go to sleep right here on this rock."

"Come on, then." He turned on his flashlight and offered his arm, which she took. Earlier he'd sensed her unease about sharing a tent. But he felt no sign of it now. They were both too tired to be tempted by anything except a good night's rest.

Reaching the tent, he unzipped the flap. The two sleeping bags had been laid out on the floor, with little more than a foot of space between them. "Go ahead," he said, holding up the flap. "I'll wait out here while you get out of your clothes and into your sleeping bag."

"Don't bother. I'm too tired to undress." She ducked inside, kicked off her sneakers and hung her damp socks from one of the tent supports. By the time Buck followed her inside, she'd crawled into her sleeping bag and pulled the top up past her ears. If she wasn't asleep yet, she was making a good show of it.

The night was pleasantly warm. Without bothering to undress, Buck slipped off his boots and stretched out on top of his sleeping bag. He'd expected to drift right off, but his thoughts wouldn't let him rest. He remembered how Terri had felt in his arms tonight, how she'd clung to him, quivering like a small, scared animal while she cracked lame jokes to hide her fear.

She was amazing—stubborn, brave, sexy and so

beautiful that Buck could scarcely believe he'd taken her for granted all these years.

When she'd looked up at him, it had been all he could do to keep from kissing her. Wisely, she'd pulled away. Kissing Terri would have been a mistake. After making love to her, and fighting the urge to do it again, a single kiss would only have left him frustrated, wanting something he could never let himself have again.

Buck was hiding a secret, one he'd kept from her since Steve's death eleven years ago. That secret alone, if it came out, would be enough to drive her away from him forever.

Buck's voice woke Terri at dawn the next morning. She opened her eyes to find him bending over her in the tent with a cup of steaming black coffee in his hand.

"Good morning." He was annoyingly bright-eyed and cheerful. "How'd you sleep?"

She sat up, finger-raking the tangles out of her hair. "Like death. Did I snore?"

"No comment." He grinned, stubble-chinned and handsome even at this ungodly hour. "Here, I brought something to wake you up." He handed her the coffee. "Careful, it's hot."

"Thanks." She took a careful sip and felt the lovely, caffeinated heat trickling down her throat. "Are our guests awake?"

"Not yet. I figured I'd give you a head start on the latrine. Ladies first."

"Thanks again. I don't suppose you have an extra toothbrush. My mouth tastes like roadkill."

"Actually, I do. I grabbed it from the gift shop when I realized I was going to have to hijack you to replace Arnie."

"I'll take it now, with toothpaste on it, please."

"Coming up."

Terri sipped her coffee, watching him as he rummaged in his dry bag. How long had it been since she was last on the river with Buck? The business had gotten so big, her own job so demanding, that she'd forgotten what it was like—the coolness of morning, bird calls blending with the sound of the current, and the first taste of fresh, hot coffee. She was rumpled, dirty and facing another strenuous day at the tiller. But right at this moment, life was good.

She would miss times like this when she left her job. But she hadn't changed her mind about going.

An hour later they were on the water. Here the canyon was narrower and deeper, its walls towering on both sides of the river. The current was swift, the rapids wild and treacherous. It took all Terri's skill to maneuver the raft through the tumbling, pitching water. Wave after wave broke over the bow, drenching everyone on board.

The four sheikhs alternately whooped with excitement and clung to the rope lines in fear for their lives. After Terri negotiated an especially challenging stretch of rapids, the men broke into applause. For a woman, especially, it was no small thing to be earning their respect. Terri caught Buck's eye. He gave her a grin and a thumbs-up.

His approval warmed her—but she'd earned it by being good at her job, Terri reminded herself. She was Buck's right-hand woman, and loving him would never be enough to change that.

Late in the afternoon, with the sun sinking below the high canyon rim, they reached calmer water. The smell of wood smoke and barbecue, wafting upriver on the breeze, told them they were nearing their camping place.

It had been a decent day, Buck observed. And Terri had done a great job. She had to be feeling good about the way she'd impressed the clients. But would it be enough to make a difference in her plan to leave?

Twenty minutes later they dragged the raft onto the sand and stumbled—cold, hungry and exhausted—into camp. Even Abdul was subdued. Hopefully he'd be too worn out to complain or make Terri uncomfortable. If the man stepped out of line one more time, Buck wouldn't hesitate to put him in his place.

A hearty meal of barbecued beef, baked beans, potatoes and skillet cornbread revived their spirits, but by the time the meal was done and Eli had serenaded them with a couple of songs, the sheikhs were trudging off to their tents to get ready for bed.

Buck helped Eli and George clear away the meal

and stash the gear. Terri had wandered off toward the river. Buck had seen Abdul go into his tent, but he still didn't like the idea of her being alone. Leaving the boys, he followed the way she'd gone.

He spotted her sitting on a rock at the river's edge, gazing out across the water. Watching her from behind, he was struck by how lonely she looked. Terri had been with him for ten years. In that time, beautiful and smart as she was, she'd never had a serious relationship with a man. She'd been there for her work, for her grandmother—and for him.

Sensing his presence, she glanced around and saw him. He raised his hand in silent greeting, then came forward and took a place beside her. For a few moments they sat without speaking as the peace of the river flowed around them. Nighthawks swooped and darted, catching insects in the moonlight. The distant call of a coyote echoed down the canyon. Terri's hands fingered a pebble.

"Are you all right, Terri?" he asked her.

"Fine." She tossed the pebble into the river. "I just needed a little time to wind down."

"Am I intruding?"

She gave a slight shake of her head. Maybe she just wanted to be still, Buck thought. But this might be his best chance to talk with her.

"You're so quiet," he said. "What are you thinking?"

"The same old thing. Just worrying about what we left behind—work issues, my grandmother and Quinn—especially Quinn." She turned toward him.

"You shouldn't have gone off and left her without saying goodbye, Buck. Quinn adores you. She needs you more than she lets on. Nobody can take your place, not Mrs. Calloway, not even me."

He scuffed a foot in the sand. "I've been planning to spend more time with her. And I will, when we get back."

"Planning isn't the same as doing. You don't even need to be here. You came because you wanted to interest those sheikhs in that new resort plan. Buck—" She laid a hand on his arm. "Why on earth do you need a new project? You're already too busy to make time for the most important person in your life—your little girl. And Quinn's growing up. One day she'll be on her own and it'll be too late to have a relationship with her." Her grip tightened. "You've built a great business and done a lot for the town. Why isn't that enough? Why can't you let go and make time for what really matters?"

The woman knew where to jab. Buck gazed at the river shimmering in the moonlight, knowing her question made sense but unsure of his answer. "You knew me growing up," he said. "The poorest kid in town, with a mother who waited tables and turned tricks at the truck stop. Maybe I had to work to get past that. And when I became successful, maybe I couldn't stop. It was the only thing that made me feel worth something. How's that for an answer?"

There was more, he realized. It involved making

up for the way Steve had died. But he wasn't going to tell her that.

"Have you ever forgiven your mother?" she asked.

"I don't know." It was as honest an answer as he could give.

"She loved you, Buck. What she did—sacrificing her pride, her reputation—she did to keep food on the table and a roof over your head. But maybe you felt like you had to be better than where you came from."

And maybe he'd shut down emotionally because he'd felt that the mother who'd birthed and raised him hadn't deserved his love.

But then, damn it, he hadn't come out here to be psychoanalyzed.

"Don't quit, Terri," he said. "I need your help. The season, the gala and Quinn, too—I can't handle all that without you. I'll raise your salary, give you stock in the company, cover your grandmother's care, beat any offer that's out there. Name it and it's yours. Just don't go."

She stood, her face in shadow. "It's too late for that, Buck. I've already made up my mind. And now, if you'll excuse me, I'm going to sleep. Don't wake me when you come to bed."

As she turned away, the moonlight caught a glimmer of tears.

Hands thrust into his pockets, Buck watched from a distance as she disappeared inside the tent. Blast it, he'd done everything but beg on his knees, but it hadn't worked. Terri seemed more determined to go than ever.

What was he going to do without her?

The third day of the run tended to be the most taxing. Today, in the sweltering, tropical heat of the lower canyon, Terri's unwashed clothes felt sweat-glued to her body. Her hair was stiff with its dried coating of muddy water. Worse, she was nearing the time for her period to start. Since it often came early, she could only cross her fingers and hope Mother Nature would hold off her monthly visit till the party reached the lodges and shops on the rim.

The canyon here had taken on a bleak moonscape quality, with the river rushing between walls of dark gray basalt that dated from the early creation of the earth. There was no shade here, few plants, no visible animals and no refuge from the burning sun.

It was a relief when, at last, the sun went down, the canyon opened up and the raft reached the last night's campsite. Except for the usual griping from Abdul and some jokes about the canyon being hotter than Dubai, the sheikhs had borne up well. But everybody was sweaty, tired and ready for the trip to end tomorrow.

As the clients trooped up the bank to collapse in folding lawn chairs and gulp cold drinks, Terri stayed behind to help Buck pull the raft higher and secure the line to a boulder.

Buck had been his usual cheerful self, but even he

seemed frayed around the edges today. Terri couldn't help wondering if she was the cause of it.

"At least we should have a calm farewell party," she said. "Nobody has enough energy to complain, not even Abdul."

"Lord, let's hope so." Buck held out his free hand to help her up the slope. "Come on. Let's get some dinner and some rest."

She took his hand and let him pull her up. It wasn't fair, she groused silently. With his mussed hair, rumpled clothes and stubbly beard, Buck still managed to look like a romance cover model. While she looked more like a drowned rat.

Dinner was grilled chicken with asparagus, roast potatoes and a bottle of alcohol-free champagne, meant for farewell toasts. But no one seemed up for toasting. The bubbly liquid was simply drunk. By the time they'd finished, it was getting dark. Clouds were rolling over the high canyon rim.

Tonight it was George's turn to entertain. In his melodious voice, accompanied by the rhythms he beat on his painted buckskin drum, he told stories of animals and how, according to legend, things had come about in the beginning of time. Most clients enjoyed George's stories. But the sheikhs were yawning before he was half-finished. In the middle of a tale, Abdul interrupted with a sharp clap of his hands.

"Enough!" he said imperiously. "How can we call this a party without a dancing girl? You, boy. Give me your drum."

George's face was expressionless, but Terri could sense the tension in him as he hesitated, then handed the man the drum, which, Terri knew, had been in his family for generations. With his long, manicured fingers, Abdul began beating out a sensual rhythm. "Now you." His gaze fixed on Terri, who sat next to Buck. "Stand up. Dance for us."

This was too much. Terri's temper rose to the boiling point. She was about to jump up and give the man a piece of her mind when Buck rose to his feet, quivering with too-long-restrained outrage. "Terri isn't your dancing girl," he said in a glacial voice. "And that drum isn't yours to play. Here." He strode to the far side of the fire, snatched the drum away, returned it to George's hands and turned back to face Abdul. "Maybe this is how you treat people where you come from. But in this country, especially on my trips, every person has the right to be treated with respect."

Picking up a five-gallon bucket of river water, he poured it on the fire, dousing the flames. "We're done here," he said. "Go back to your tents and get ready to be on the river by sunup. We should be at Phantom Ranch before noon. From there, you can plan on a five-hour mule ride to the top.

As if to underscore his words, he took the half-empty bottle of nonalcoholic champagne and poured it on the smoking ashes. "I mean it," he said. "We're done."

Buck sat in a lawn chair next to the doused fire pit, stirring the ashes with a stick to check for live coals.

As expected, he found none, but at least it gave him something to do.

Everyone else, including Terri, had gone to bed, but Buck was too wired to sleep. This would be his last night in the canyon with Terri. He'd hoped that in the peaceful beauty of this place, he could talk her out of quitting her job. But nothing had gone right. Now she seemed more determined to leave than ever.

Exhausted by the long, hot day and upset by the scene with Abdul, she'd turned in early. Knowing his restlessness would keep her awake, Buck had stayed up, prowling the camp and waiting for his nerves to calm. At last he'd settled in a chair, resolving to stay until he could get to sleep without disturbing Terri.

His head had begun to droop when he was startled by a faint but unmistakable sound—the opening of a metal tent zipper. Peering toward the tents, he could make out a moving figure. It was too tall to be Terri and it didn't appear to be Eli or George. It had to be one of the sheikhs.

As Buck watched, the man hesitated, then turned and walked straight toward him.

"Good evening." It was Omar, the quietest of the four. Compared to the others, he seemed almost shy, perhaps because he spoke halting, schoolbook English.

"Good evening to you, Omar." Buck rose and greeted him politely. "Is there something I can do for you?"

"Please sit," Omar said. "I was hoping for this chance to speak to you alone."

Buck sat down again and waited for Omar to pull up a nearby camp stool. "What is it?" he asked, bracing for more complaints. "Is something wrong?"

Omar leaned closer, his voice dropping. "I want to apologize for my friend Abdul. The man is like a brother to me. But I am not proud of how he has treated you, your staff or your woman. We are guests in your country. Guests do not behave this way. I might have corrected my friend, but that would have offended him. For that, too, I must apologize."

Buck thought back over the past three days. He could dismiss the complaining. But Abdul's behavior toward Terri was unconscionable.

"Maybe you should apologize to Miss Hammond," he said. "She was forced to come on this trip when one of the men couldn't make it. She's done a fine job, but if I'd known how your friend was going to treat her, I would never have brought her along."

"I am truly sorry for that. But I fear that an apology to her face might be awkward, both for her and for me. Perhaps, since she is your woman, you could apologize for us."

"I will give her your apology," Buck said. "But she's not really my woman. She's my employee and my friend—and very much her own woman."

"But you share a tent."

"Only because we have to. Believe me, there's nothing going on in there but sleep."

A smile tugged at the corners of Omar's mouth. "In that case, you must be a very foolish man. A woman like that—so beautiful, so strong, with so much spirit—how could you not give her the attention and appreciation she deserves?"

"That—" Buck sighed as he rose to his feet "—is a very long story."

"Too long for the late hour, perhaps." Omar rose with him and extended his hand. "I will bid you goodnight."

Buck accepted the man's handshake and watched as he made his way back to his tent and ducked inside. Yawning now, he shook his head. He had a lot to learn about people and their natures. But right now, if he didn't get some sleep, he'd be dead on his feet tomorrow.

He was debating whether he should give Terri more time when a lightning bolt cracked across the sky, followed by a deafening thunderclap. The clouds split open, pouring a deluge of rain down into the canyon.

Six

Buck's first impulse was to rush to the shelter of the tent. But the rafts were loosely tethered on the riverbank, just above the waterline. The camp was safe on high ground, but if the rain caused the river to rise, the rafts could be swept away, leaving the group stranded here.

His crew recognized the danger. George and Eli burst out of their tent and joined Buck in the wild race to the river. Terri, appearing out of nowhere, was right behind them, running barefoot through the storm.

Leaping and sliding down the muddy slope to the bank, they reached the rafts and grabbed the ropes, George and Eli on the gear raft, Buck and Terri on the client raft. The river was already rising from flash floods upstream. Muddy water swirled around their ankles, the current tugging at the rafts. Minutes later, it might have been too late.

Bracing and pulling with all their strength, they managed to drag the rafts to safety and secure the lines around the heavy boulders that littered the upper bank. It hadn't taken long. But by the time it was done, all four were drenched and exhausted.

The rain had slowed to a misty drizzle. As George and Eli headed back to their tent, Buck gave Terri his hand to help her up the slippery bank. She was soaked to the skin. Her khakis clung to her body, cold-puckered nipples showing through her shirt. Her hair framed her face in dripping strings. The night air was warm, but the river water had been frigid. She was so cold her teeth were chattering.

"Come on, let's get you warm." Buck circled her with an arm, feeling her body shiver against him. "You didn't need to come out here in the storm, Terri. I could've managed the rafts with the boys."

"Could you?" She fell into step beside him. "What if you couldn't? We might've lost a raft and everything in it. I was doing my job, just as Arnie would've done if he'd been here." She was silent for a moment, limping a little as they moved toward the tent. "What was Arnie's problem, anyway? You never told me why I had to take his place. You just said he couldn't make it."

The guilt that stabbed Buck's conscience was too sharp to ignore. He'd told Terri enough lies. She deserved the truth—about this, at least.

"I have a confession to make," he said. "I switched Arnie's schedule because I wanted *you* on this trip. You'd just told me you were quitting. I wanted some time with you before you left, away from the chaos of the office—I was hoping I could change your mind."

She'd stiffened against him, still shivering. "You know I don't like being manipulated, Buck."

"I know. But I really wanted you to have a good time."

"You could've just asked me."

"Would you have said yes?"

"Probably not. I've worried the whole three days about what I left behind." She stumbled against him, wincing.

"What's wrong? Did you hurt your foot?"

"It's just a sticker. I can get it out."

They'd reached the tent. He raised the flap for her to duck inside, then followed her. "Sit," he said, reaching for his flashlight and switching it on. "I'll have a look at that foot."

Terri didn't argue. Still dripping, she lowered herself to the space on the floor of the tent. Buck wiped the mud off her feet with a towel from his bag. It was easy to find the cactus spine that was stuck in the ball of her foot, but it was in deep. She gave a little yelp as he pulled it out.

"Are you okay?" He sponged away a drop of blood, then salved the spot with the antibiotic cream he kept in his kit.

She nodded. "Just cold."

"You can't sleep in those wet clothes. You'll need to hang them up to dry."

"I know. You, too." She hesitated. Her show of modesty was ludicrous, since he remembered the sight of her, half-naked and straddling his hips. But they both seemed to have decided not to mention that.

"Here." He switched off the flashlight, leaving the tent in darkness. "For privacy, that's the best I can do. You first. I'll give you some space."

He moved back into a corner of the tent, crouching in the cramped space as he listened to the small sounds of Terri getting undressed—the slide of a zipper, the rustle of bunching fabric, the little grunt of effort as she peeled her wet pants over her hips. The mental picture was enough to bring him to full arousal. He battled the urge to seize her in his arms for a repeat performance of that morning in his room. This wasn't the time or place. The tent was too small, its walls too thin and it was too close to neighbors. If he made love to Terri again—and the need to make that happen was driving him crazy—he wanted to do it right.

She draped her clothes on the tent frame, then snuggled down into her sleeping bag. "All clear," she said.

Buck felt chilled, too. He stripped off his clothes, hung them up and crawled into bed. They lay side by side, zipped into their sleeping bags, both of them still too charged with adrenaline to sleep. Realizing she was awake, Buck decided to take a chance.

"Should I apologize for this trip?" he asked. "I had good intentions, but I know it's been rough on you."

She rolled over to face him in the darkness. "There's no need to apologize for the trip. I enjoyed the good parts and survived the bad. What I'm unhappy about is that you lied to get me here."

"I know. But I was desperate to bring you. Since I knew you wouldn't come willingly, it was either tell a fib or tie you up and throw you on the raft."

"No comment."

Waiting for Terri to say more, Buck studied the faint outline of her face in the darkness. He remembered watching her today on the river, as the breeze fluttered a strand of chestnut hair across her sunfreckled face. Even after a third day of roughing it on the river, she was beautiful—not like the pampered women he usually dated, but strong and graceful like a wild mare or a soaring hawk. He'd always thought she was pretty. But not until this topsy-turvy week had he realized how magnificent she was.

Was it too late to stop himself from falling in love with her?

For years, he'd told himself that Terri was off-limits as anything but a friend. She was Steve's sister, and he'd promised to care for her like family. But she'd broken out of that box, and he could no longer deny the power of his growing feelings for her.

Don't go, Terri. Stay here. Give us a chance to see what might happen.

Buck knew better than to say the words. Terri deserved a better life than she'd found in Porter Hollow as his right-hand woman. If she wanted to go and find it, who was he to stop her—especially since she'd already made up her mind to leave?

She'd fallen silent. "Are you getting sleepy?" he asked.

"A little. But I'm still cold." Her teeth chattered faintly as she spoke.

"Come here." Impulsively, he grabbed a fistful of her sleeping bag and pulled her against him. Terri didn't resist. Wrapped chastely in a cocoon of nylon and synthetic down, she nestled her rump into the curve of his body and let him wrap his arms around her. Within minutes her breathing told Buck she'd drifted off to sleep.

As he lay with his arm across her shoulders, the tingle of awareness became an ache, deepening the urge to move above her and taste those soft lips. He imagined unzipping her sleeping bag, cradling a satiny breast in his palm and stroking her nipple until she moaned.

But as long as he was fantasizing, why stop there? He could imagine being someplace else, someplace private, clean and warm where he could scoop her up in his arms and carry her to bed, where they could relive their single bedroom encounter over and over till they were both deliciously sated.

Was Terri having similar dreams? She'd climbed into his bed once. Surely she wouldn't be averse to doing it a second time, and more...

Buck's thoughts had triggered his arousal again. Imagining an ice-cold shower, he brought himself under a measure of control. Tomorrow they'd be back in their familiar world, slipping into their roles as boss and employee as they counted the days till her departure. The more he thought about it, the less he looked forward to it.

How could he let her walk away without taking one last chance?

By the time they reached the South Rim tomorrow they'd be sore, hungry, tired—and within a few minutes' walk of a comfortable lodge with a good restaurant. They'd both be ready for showers, a good meal and a night's rest before driving back to Porter Hollow in the company vehicle that waited for them. The possibilities were…intriguing, to say the least.

Holding that thought and cradling Terri close, Buck drifted off to sleep.

Phantom Ranch, at the bottom of the Grand Canyon's inner gorge, was a cluster of picturesque stone cabins and a small lodge with beds that could be reserved by hikers, river runners and mule riders for a night's rest. Here Terri, Buck and the four sheikhs gathered their personal gear and left the raft to be towed downriver by George and Eli.

Terri stood on the riverbank, watching the two rafts disappear around the bend. She would ask to make sure the clients had tipped the hard-working camp boys. If not, she would suggest to Buck that he pay them a generous bonus. They'd earned it on this trip.

By the time the group had taken advantage of the restroom and enjoyed snacks at the cantina, the mule train had arrived to take them up the winding trail to the rim. Terri had hiked that trail—a grueling eight-hour climb—several times in the past. Today she was grateful for the mule ride, which would cut the time by nearly half. She was hot, filthy and anxious to get back to her normal routine.

They mounted up and headed out at a plodding, swaying walk. There were seven big brown mules including one for the driver, who took the lead. Buck brought up the rear with Terri in front of him, and the sheikhs were strung out between. Riding single file on the narrow trail, there wouldn't be much chance to talk, which was fine. She needed some quiet time to regroup for whatever awaited her back in Porter Hollow.

She was sharply aware of Buck riding behind her, but she was too emotionally raw to turn and give him a look or a word. Last night in the canyon, he'd been so kind and protective that she'd almost believed he could care for her. But back in the real world, she knew Buck was bound to become as demanding and insensitive as ever.

The person she'd been a week ago would have patiently followed Buck's orders and accepted being taken for granted as her due. But now she knew she didn't have to be a doormat for any man—not even the high-and-mighty Buck Morgan.

The air in the deep gorge was like a sauna. By the end of the first hour, Terri was dripping. She swigged from the furnished canteen to stay hydrated. At least the higher portion of the trail would be cooler. But looking up from here, the next three hours up a steep, winding trail couldn't be over soon enough.

By the time the mule train wound its way onto the rim of the canyon, the sun was low, the air fresh and pleasant. While Buck tipped the mule driver, the four sheikhs, muddied, bone-weary and sore, climbed off their mounts and staggered toward the limousine that waited to take them to the lodge.

Terri stood with Buck at the trailhead and watched the limo drive away. "At last," Buck muttered.

"Amen," Terri echoed. "By the way, I forgot to ask. What's our plan for getting home?"

"The SUV that Kirby drove here with the sheikhs' luggage should be waiting for us behind the lodge. Since Kirby will be going as steward on the jet tomorrow, you and I will be driving the vehicle back. Are you hungry? We could have dinner before we leave, or even check in, clean up and get a good night's sleep. How does that sound to you?"

Tempting, Terri thought. She knew what would likely happen if they stayed the night. The question was, did she want another no-strings-attached romp with Buck? One that, like the last time, would lead nowhere and mean nothing?

"Let me think about that while I run to the rest-room," she said. "Maybe you should call and let some-body know we're here."

"Fine." Buck whipped out his cell phone. "It's al-most five. With luck there'll still be somebody in the office. If not, at least I can pick up any messages on my landline."

"You might want to call your house, too. Quinn will want to know you're on your way back."

She left him and strode off to the nearby stone building that housed the restrooms. Before leaving, she took time to splash the dusty sweat residue from her face, neck and arms and slick back her hair. She looked like forty miles of bad road—or bad river. She didn't have a change of clothes, or even a credit card to buy something clean in the gift shop or one of the tourist boutiques. Maybe she and Buck could order room service if she agreed to stay the night.

If she agreed to stay the night? Was she really con-sidering it? What about her pride?

Still uncertain, she walked outside to find Buck waiting for her. The look on his face stopped her in her tracks. Her pulse lurched. Something was wrong.

"What is it?" she asked. "Did you reach anybody at the office? Is everything all right?"

"I spoke with Bob. Everything at the office is fine."

"Did you call Quinn?"

"I called the house. Nobody answered so I left a message." He drew a sharp breath. "Terri—"

In the silence that hung between them, she felt cold dread crawling up her spine. "Tell me," she said.

"It's your grandmother. She passed away two days ago."

Buck watched the color fade from Terri's face. She'd loved her grandmother. The loss would cut her deeply. But even more painful, and more lasting, would be the regret that she hadn't been there to comfort the old woman in her final moments—and say goodbye.

For that, Buck had nobody to blame but himself.

She hadn't spoken a word. She didn't have to. Her anguished expression said it all. No thanks to him, she'd wasted three days on the river and, in a time of dire need, failed her beloved grandma, the woman who'd been like a mother to her.

"I'm sorry, Terri." The words fell pathetically short of what he wanted to say.

"I need to get home now. Let's go." Turning away from him, she strode off in the direction of where their vehicle would be waiting. Her spine was rigid, her shoulders painfully square.

Buck trailed a few steps behind her. If she never spoke to him again, he wouldn't blame her. But between here and Porter Hollow they had more than a two-hour drive ahead of them. Maybe he could at least get her to talk. Even railing at him, which he deserved, would be better for them both than this stony silence.

He needed to hear her words as much as she needed to say them.

* * *

The tan SUV with the Bucket List logo on the door was parked near the hotel's back entrance, its key under the mat where Kirby, the jet steward, had left it. Without a word, Terri climbed into the passenger seat, fastened her seat belt and opened one of the chilled water bottles Kirby had left in the console. She sipped the water in silence as Buck climbed into the driver's seat, buckled up and started the engine.

Twenty minutes later they'd left the park behind and were headed up Highway 89, which would take them north through the Navajo reservation to Page, across the bridge at Glen Canyon and from there over the Utah border to Porter Hollow. In the west, the sky above the desert blazed with a fiery sunset. By the time they got home it would be dark.

Buck stole a glance at Terri's stubborn profile. She was gazing out the side window, still not speaking. The two of them had had their ups and downs over the past ten years, but never a week as tumultuous as this one. Whatever came of it, good or bad, Buck sensed that their relationship would never be the same as before.

The silence between them was like rising water, threatening to fill the breathing space and drown them both. Unable to stand it any longer, Buck spoke.

"Are you all right, Terri?"

"That depends on your definition of *all right*." She spoke without turning to look at him. "The one thing I could have done for my grandma was be there for her.

I couldn't even manage that because I was *working*—trying to keep you and your billionaire clients happy."

"I know. I'm sorry." Buck knew his reply was lame, but it was all he could offer.

"How did she die?" Terri asked. "Did Bob tell you? Was she in the hospital? In her chair?"

"I don't think Bob knew. He only told me she'd passed away."

She exhaled, slumping in the seat. Outside, the darkness was closing around them. "Well, I guess I'll find out when I get home. And I guess I'll have a funeral service to plan. I hope you won't mind giving me a couple of days off."

"Take all the time you need," Buck said. "In fact, I want to pay for your grandmother's funeral. I know you've been paying for her care at Canyon Shadows. You can't have a lot of cash to spare."

There was a long pause before she spoke. "Why would you do that?" she demanded. "Do you think you owe me?"

Buck caught the cold anger in her voice. "It's my fault you missed being there for her," he said. "I'd like to make amends if I can."

"With *money*?" She jerked around to face him. "This isn't about money, Buck. It's about love and family duty. I will pay for my grandmother's funeral, and I don't want a nickel from you!"

Buck held his tongue, hoping she was finished. Maybe it had been crass, offering to pay for the funeral. But damn it, he'd meant well. Couldn't she give him credit for that?

"You think money's the answer to everything, don't you?" The words spilled out of her like water through a broken dam. "Even with Quinn—you're too busy to spend time with her, so you whip out your credit card and buy her whatever she wants, as if that makes everything all right. As for me—you pay me the salary I earn. That's enough—all I expect. I don't need your charity for the funeral or anything else." She finished off her water and crushed the thin plastic bottle between her hands. "As long as we're on the subject, what was it that prompted you to put sixteen hundred dollars' worth of new tires on my Jeep? Was that some kind of misplaced guilt, too? For what?"

Buck felt the sting. She was cutting too close to a nerve. But he was a captive audience. He couldn't just stop the vehicle and walk away without answering.

"All right," he said. "Since you asked, I might as well tell you. When we were in Iraq, I promised Steve that if anything happened to him, I'd look after you. Lately I've realized that apart from giving you a job, I haven't done much to live up to that promise. So when you needed new tires, I wanted to help. That's all."

It wasn't all. Not by a long shot. But Terri was upset enough. For now it was as much as she could handle.

But she kept pushing him, getting under his skin. "I was in my teens when you and Steve enlisted. I'm a grown woman now. Damn it, Buck, I don't need looking after, especially when you do it all out of guilt!"

"Fine. Message received loud and clear."

Jaw set, hands gripping the wheel, Buck could feel his temper boiling over. The river run had been a lousy waste of time. He was filthy, unshaven, hungry and exhausted, and now this fool woman had not only rejected his well-meant offer of help, but she'd dismissed his motive as guilt.

What the hell, she was partially right. But that didn't mean he had to take being treated like the bad guy—not when she wasn't exactly Little Miss Innocent herself.

The words came out before he could think to stop them.

"As long as we're asking questions, tell me what the devil you were doing in my bed the morning I was sick. I remember it being a lot of fun, but not much else."

As soon as Buck heard her gasp he knew he'd made a serious mistake. He willed himself to focus his eyes on the road. There could be no taking back what he'd just said. All he could do was brazen it out and deal with the consequences.

"How dare you?" she sputtered.

"*How dare I?* Stop acting like a character out of some damned Jane Austen novel. I was half-drugged out of my mind, and you took advantage of me."

Another gasp. "*I* took advantage? I leaned over the bed to make sure you were all right. You grabbed my hand and put it on your...never mind. I've been trying to make myself believe it never happened. A gentleman would never have brought it up."

"You've known me most of your life. Have I ever claimed to be a gentleman? It happened, Terri, and I'm sick of pretending it didn't."

"Is that why you bought the tires for my Jeep? Because I slept with you?"

"Lord, no. I can't believe you'd think that."

Terri didn't reply. When he risked a glance at her, she was staring out the front window, her jaw stubbornly set. Should he apologize? But no, she was past listening. His words would most likely set off another tirade. Besides, he was glad to have it out in the open, so he didn't have to ignore what had happened between them anymore.

But right or wrong, he'd turned a dangerous corner with Terri. Their once-comfortable relationship would never be the same. And now, especially with her grandmother gone, she'd probably be eager to leave Porter Hollow—and him.

He'd been in denial about her leaving, Buck realized. Maybe he still was. Either way, he wasn't ready to deal with losing her.

Terri watched the headlights sweep past the broken yellow lines on the highway. Here and there, in the darkness, specks of light from Navajo homes glowed like distant stars. A big double-trailer truck, roaring past in the southbound lane, left the air tinged with diesel fumes.

She willed herself not to think. Her mind was too tired to process all that had happened and come to any kind of intelligent conclusion. She knew only that the course of her life had just taken a drastic turn. She'd always counted on her grandmother, her job and Buck to provide her with stability. Now it was as if she was standing on a crumbling precipice, about to tumble into thin air.

Buck had turned on the radio, but most of the stations on the dial were nothing but static. Only an annoying call-in talk show came through clearly. After a few minutes Buck turned it off. The silence was even more oppressive than before, but it was as if they both knew talking would only do more damage. This was the first time in Terri's memory that she and Buck had nothing to say to each other.

Ahead, she could see the bright lights of Page and the Glen Canyon Dam. Buck slowed for the town. "I could use some coffee. Want something?"

At least he was talking. "No thanks," Terri said. "I think I'll just crawl into the back and try to sleep. If I'm still out when we get back to Porter Hollow, let me off at the hotel. My Jeep and my purse should be there."

"Fine." That was all he said. Terri waited till the SUV pulled up to a drive-through window. Then she crawled over the console and onto the backseat. Somebody had left a thin fleece blanket there. Curling up in it, she closed her eyes. She was too agitated to sleep, she told herself. But at least if she pretended to, she and Buck wouldn't have to worry about talking—or not talking.

The SUV pulled out of the drive-through and headed back to the highway. For all her frayed nerves, Terri was exhausted. It took only minutes for the purr of the engine and the gentle vibration beneath her body to lull her into dreamless sleep.

Seven

"Wake up, Terri. We're here."

Roused by Buck's voice, Terri pushed herself upright in the backseat. Through the side windows of the SUV, she could see the familiar lights that marked the back entrance to the hotel. As she blinked herself awake, the turmoil of the past few hours refocused in her mind. No, it hadn't been a bad dream. Her beloved grandma was gone, and Buck had finally brought up the morning they'd had sex.

Whether she was ready or not, it was time to face reality.

"Your Jeep's across the parking lot," he said. "Want me to stay until you get your keys and make sure the engine starts?"

She untangled herself from the blanket, opened the

back door of the SUV and stumbled out on unsteady legs. "Don't worry about it. You need to get home. I'll be fine." She closed the door hard, maybe too hard.

He rolled down the window. "I'll swing back this way after I've picked up the Hummer. If you need any help, wave."

"I said I'll be fine. I don't need you to look after me." She turned away and strode into the hotel. The hour was early, not yet nine o'clock. If the Jeep wouldn't start, there were other people she could ask for help.

The concierge had her purse, tucked into a drawer. "That must've been some trip," the woman said, looking her up and down.

Terri faked a grin. "You can't imagine. I'll tell you about it later. Thanks for keeping an eye on this." She took her purse and left the way she'd come in. Buck was gone, but her Jeep started on the first try. With a sigh of relief, she pulled out of the parking lot. All she really felt like doing was going home, stripping down for a long, hot, soapy shower and crawling into bed. But some things couldn't wait.

She would call Canyon Shadows, let them know she was back and find out everything she could about her grandmother. If they needed her to stop by in person or go to the mortuary right away, she'd drive straight there. The way she looked wasn't important.

Terri pulled the Jeep to the curb, fished in her purse and found her cell phone. She'd forgotten to turn it off before handing over her purse, and after being left on for three days without a charge, the battery was dead. With an impatient mutter, she stuffed the phone back in her purse. Never mind, she'd just go straight on to Canyon Shadows and begin the sad business of laying her grandmother to rest.

Starting the Jeep again, Terri pulled into the evening traffic. Harriet Cooper had been ready to go— no question of that. But she'd deserved better than to die alone or among cold-eyed strangers. For the rest of her life Terri would regret that she hadn't been there for the woman who'd given her so much.

Buck turned onto the road that wound up the canyon to his home. He thought about calling the house again, to let Quinn and Mrs. Calloway know he was coming. But it hardly seemed worth the trouble when he'd be there in a few minutes.

Earlier, no one had answered his call. But that had been almost three hours ago. If they'd gone out for dinner, by now they should be home. He could just walk in and surprise his daughter. Maybe, once he'd showered and changed, he could even take her out for ice cream and catch up.

Terri's Jeep had been gone when he'd driven back through the parking lot. She'd been anxious to get away from him. For that he could hardly blame her. Tonight the trust they'd built over the years had shattered. Healing, if even possible, would be long and painful, but Buck wasn't ready to give up. For now he would allow her some space, let her get through the process of grieving for her grandmother. Maybe after that he'd have a chance of winning her back.

Whatever it took, if there was any way to keep her from leaving, he had to try.

Rounding the last curve in the road, he could see his house, every window lit. Apprehension trailed a cold finger up his spine. The feeling that something was wrong became a certainty as he drove through the open gate and saw the county sheriff's brown Toyota Land Cruiser parked next to the house.

Heart pounding, Buck braked the Hummer, sprang to the ground and raced up the porch steps. Had there been a break-in? Was Quinn all right?

Mrs. Calloway met him at the door. Her face was pale, her eyes bloodshot.

"What is it?" he asked, sick with dread.

"It's Quinn. She's gone missing."

Buck forced himself to speak past the shock. "What happened?"

"After lunch she said she was going to her room to play games on her computer. I checked on her at two. She wasn't there."

"There's no sign of her in the house and no evidence of a struggle." The sheriff, a bear of a man whose belly strained the buttons on his uniform, lumbered down the stairs to face Buck. "I'd say it looks more like a runaway than a kidnapping."

"But as my daughter, she'd be a target for kidnappers. Have you issued an Amber Alert?" Buck demanded.

The sheriff shook his head. "That's a pretty drastic measure. I don't want to do that and then find out she just wandered off."

Buck clenched his jaw, biting back an angry outburst. It wouldn't help to antagonize the man. He tried to pull himself together, forcing himself to think logically. "Did she take anything? Any food? Any clothes?" he asked.

Mrs. Calloway shook her head. "No food. I'm not sure about anything else. There's plenty of clothes left in her closet. I wouldn't know if something was missing." Her eyes welled with tears. "Oh, Lord, Mr. Morgan, I'm sorry. I don't know what happened. I watched that girl like a hawk!"

"It wasn't your fault. Just help us find her. Think— what did she do? What did she say before you missed her?"

"She said she was bored. But she was always saying that."

"What about the dog?" Buck asked the sheriff.

"The dog's here. He's fine."

"And you didn't hear him barking, Mrs. Calloway?"

"No. Didn't hear a thing all afternoon—and I was wide-awake, just watching TV."

"For now I have to assume the girl left on her own," the sheriff said. "Maybe she just went to a friend's house. Maybe you should try calling around."

Buck's patience was wearing thin. Why was everybody standing around talking when his little girl could be in danger? "She doesn't have friends here," he said. "She just came for the summer."

"What about somebody she might've met online? Like a boy? Or even somebody *pretending* to be a boy?" The implication was clear.

Buck's control snapped. "Good Lord, she's nine years old! She's not into boys yet. But if she's out there wandering around alone, anything could've happened to her! Why are we wasting time? We need to get moving and find her!"

"We're doing all we can, Mr. Morgan." The sheriff sounded like a bad imitation of a detective on a TV crime show. "I've put out an alert and given her description to my deputies. They're all watching for her. The best thing for now is sit tight and stay calm."

It was all Buck could do to keep from punching the man. "Hell, I've got a whole security team of ex-cops and ex-military at the resort. I'm calling them now to form a search party."

Buck stepped to one side and dialed Ed Clarkson, his chief of security. Clarkson, who'd once run the missing persons bureau in Tucson, promised to put every available man and woman on the search. "Most of us know your daughter, so we'll know who to look for," he said. "I'll get right on this."

"There's a school photo of Quinn in my office. You've got a key to the place. Make some copies and hand them out. And thanks, Ed." Buck paused to collect his thoughts. "I'll check her computer and call you if I find anything you need to know. Then I'll take the dog and check the canyon trails. She could've gone hiking and gotten lost or hurt."

"Good idea. I'll be in touch. Don't worry, Buck, we'll find her."

Buck ended the call, then scrolled down to Terri's number. Terri was dealing with a lot right now. But he had to bring her into this. She loved Quinn and would be concerned about her. She might even have some idea where the girl would have gone.

He tried the number. Nothing. If Terri had left her phone on during the river run, it made sense that the battery would be dead. Feeling strangely alone without her support, Buck slipped the phone back in his pocket. He'd needed Terri—needed to hear her voice, needed to share his fears with her and know she was there for him. Now all he could do was try her again later, after she'd had time to charge her phone. Right now he needed to check Quinn's computer.

Ignoring the scowl on the sheriff's face, he hurried up the stairs and down the hall to Quinn's bedroom. The sight of her ruffled bedcover and scattered cushions, her precious stuffed animals, and her fuzzy slippers tossed on the rug triggered an ache in his throat.

Pushing the emotion aside, he found Quinn's laptop on her desk and switched it on. Buck had insisted on knowing her password—thank heaven for that. He had no trouble getting into her texts and email.

He could've saved himself the trouble. Almost all of the messages and texts involved her girlfriends in Sedona. It was the usual schoolgirl chatter—nothing alarming, nothing to indicate that she'd met anyone new or was planning to go anywhere. Even her complaints about boredom and being monitored by Mrs. Calloway came as no surprise. Buck had known how she felt. The only message that caught his eye was a recent one to her mother, sent yesterday.

Hi, Mom. Daddy's gone again, this time on the river, for days. He didn't even say goodbye. He just called Mrs. C. and told her he had to go on a river run. Terri took me shopping last week, but Daddy was too busy to even look at what we bought. At least in Sedona I have my friends. I feel like a prisoner. I hate it here.

The words ripped into Buck's heart. He loved his daughter, and he'd had good intentions about spending time with her while she was in town. But good intentions weren't enough for a little girl who needed his time and affection. If anything had happened to Quinn, he'd have only himself to blame.

Lord, what was he going to tell Diane? Their marriage might have been a disaster, but she was a decent mother. If she knew her daughter was missing she'd be out of her mind with worry.

He would spare his ex-wife until he knew more, Buck resolved. Meanwhile, he'd learned all he could from Quinn's computer. It was time to get the dog and a flashlight and search the canyon. Picking up a discarded sock off the floor, he kept it to give the dog her scent. Murphy was no trained bloodhound, but he would recognize that scent as Quinn's, and he was protective of the girl. He might at least be able to hear her if she was in trouble.

Buck had never been a praying man, but as he passed the landing to go downstairs, he paused long enough to say a silent prayer for his daughter's safety. Wherever she'd gone, he vowed, he would find her.

Terri had spent half an hour at Canyon Shadows talking to the director. Her grandmother had passed away quietly, alone in her armchair with the TV blaring an old Lawrence Welk broadcast. One of the aides had discovered her when she'd gone in to bring dinner.

"There was nothing you could have done, dear." The director was an athletic fiftyish woman with glasses and dyed red hair that clashed with her purple pantsuit. "Nothing any of us could have done. It was her time. From the looks of the dear lady, I'd say she didn't suffer. We called the mortuary over in Hurricane, the one listed on the form you filled out. They've got her in their morgue, waiting for you to come make the arrangements." Her sharp gaze took in Terri's bloodshot eyes, matted hair and muddy clothes. "I'm sure that can wait till morning, dear. You look exhausted. Go home and get some rest."

Terri shook her head. "I'd rather get things settled now. Will somebody be there at this hour?"

"If you like, I can call them and find out." She reached for the phone.

An hour later, Terri was on her way back home. The

funeral director had met her at the mortuary where she'd chosen a plain casket, arranged for a simple graveside service and paid with her credit card. The sad errand could have waited till tomorrow, but she hadn't wanted to leave it undone any longer. And if Buck decided to be "helpful," he'd be told that everything had been taken care of. She didn't need his guilt-driven charity.

Coming back into town, she turned off the main road and onto the narrow lane that led to her grandmother's neat little clapboard house—her house now, she supposed. It would make sense to sell it—the home wasn't worth much but it sat on an acre of choice land, prime for development.

Never mind, she could think about that later. Right now she was so tired she could barely hold her head up. All she wanted was to shower and pull on clean sweats, microwave the leftover lasagna in the fridge, open a beer and put her feet up.

Looking down the lane toward the house, Terri saw something that made her heart lurch. There were lights on inside, glowing through the kitchen and living room windows.

Had she forgotten to turn the lights off four days ago when she'd left to drive the truck to Lee's Ferry? It was possible, she conceded. It had been early, still dark outside, when she'd locked the house. And she'd been preoccupied, thinking about Buck. Still, it wasn't like her to go away and leave lights burning. She had

to assume that someone had broken into the house—
and that they could still be inside.

A half block from the house, she stopped the Jeep
and turned off the headlights. With a dead phone, she
couldn't call 911. She could always drive into town
and get help. But she'd feel pretty silly if it turned out
she'd left the lights on herself. She was going to need
a closer look.

Taking care not to make a sound, she climbed out
of the Jeep. There was a tire iron in the back. It wasn't
a gun, but if she ran into trouble it would be better
than no weapon at all.

She kept to the shadows as she neared the house.
Nothing inside was worth stealing—the TV and her
computer were old, her jewelry little more than odds
and ends. But some homeless person, needing food
and shelter, could have broken in. Gripping the tire
iron, she tiptoed to the kitchen window and peered
over the sill.

The light above the stove was on. There was no one
in the room, but someone had definitely been here. A
carton of milk, a bowl with a spoon in it and a box of
cereal sat on the kitchen table. The cereal was a sugary
brand that Terri didn't like. She'd bought it last year
when Quinn slept over and hadn't touched it since.

Her hand loosened its grip on the tire iron. Acting
on a hunch, Terri walked around to the back of the
house. When she and Steve were kids, they'd adopted
a small stray dog and had talked their grandmother
into installing a pet entrance in the back door. The

dog was long gone, but the swinging flap remained. The latch that held it shut would be easy to lift or break from the outside, especially for a certain little someone who had been to her house before and knew where to feel for it.

On the back porch, she crouched next to the pet door and gave it a gentle push. It swung freely. Terri began to relax.

She opened the back door with her key and walked into the kitchen. No one was there, but she could see the glow of a floor lamp in the living room. "Hello?" she called softly. No one answered.

Knowing she couldn't be too careful, she kept a grip on the tire iron as she walked into the living room. Fast asleep on the old sofa, under the crocheted afghan, was Quinn.

Terri laid the tire iron on the rug and dropped to her knees beside the sofa. Only then did she see the tearstains on Quinn's face. Buck's daughter had cried herself to sleep.

"Quinn, wake up!" Terri gave the girl's shoulder a gentle nudge.

With a little murmur, Quinn opened her eyes. "Hi, Terri," she said.

"What on earth are you doing here?" Terri was torn between hugging the girl and reading her the riot act.

Quinn sat up. "I was bored, and I wanted to see you. I thought maybe we could do something together."

"But how did you get here, Quinn? It's two or three miles, at least, from your father's house."

"I walked. I went the short way, on the old back road, but it still took me *forever*. Then you weren't here, and I was too tired to walk home. I would've called somebody to come get me, but Daddy won't let me have a phone. He says I'm not old enough."

Terri felt weak-kneed. Porter Hollow wasn't a big place, but with so many strangers around, anything could've happened to the girl. "Did you tell anybody where you were going?"

Quinn shook her head. "Mrs. C. would've stopped me. She treats me like a prisoner. Can't I stay here for a while?"

Terri rose to her feet. "Not another minute. Your dad and Mrs. Calloway will be frantic. I've got to take you home."

"Can't you just call them?" Quinn looked ready to cry again.

"I don't have a landline. My phone's dead and we don't have time to recharge it. Come on." She took Quinn's hand and pulled her up. "Did you bring anything, like a backpack?"

Lower lip jutting, Quinn shook her head. "Aren't you at least glad to see me?"

"Oh, honey, of course I am!" Terri flung her arms around the pouting child. "I'm always glad to see you."

Quinn nestled against her. "You're not mad?"

"Not a bit. Just surprised and very glad you're okay."

"Then why can't I stay?"

"Because your dad will be looking for you. He'll be worried sick. Now come on, let's get you home."

Terri locked the house and rushed Quinn out to the Jeep. Avoiding the Main Street traffic, she took the back way to the canyon turnoff. Beside her in the passenger seat, Quinn was silent. Buck's daughter probably felt she'd been betrayed—that the one friend she'd turned to was hauling her home to be punished. Attempting to explain might be a waste of breath, but Terri knew she had to try.

"You know your father loves you, don't you, Quinn?"

"Does he? Then why does he leave me alone so much?"

Because he has a company to run and he has a lot of demands on his time. That was the first reply that popped into Terri's head. But she knew it wouldn't be enough for Quinn. She had to go deeper, to find an answer that would mean something to a lonely little girl.

"You know he's busy," she said. "But I think the real reason is that he doesn't understand how much you need him—or how much he needs you."

Quinn pondered a moment. "So how do we let him know that?"

Terri had turned the Jeep onto the canyon road. Ahead she could see the lights of the house, blazing like a beacon in the night. "I'll give it some thought," she said, for want of a wiser answer. "You think about it, too. Maybe something will come to us."

The gate stood open. As she drove through, Terri could feel the tension flooding her body. After a cataclysmic fight and an awkward parting, she'd hoped for some private time to rest, recover and think about her future. But no such luck. Thanks to Quinn, she was about to face Buck again.

Buck had found no trace of Quinn in the canyon. Murphy had treated the whole outing as a romp, tugging at his leash, sniffing at squirrel holes and lifting his leg at every bend in the trail. After calling Quinn's name again and again, shining his flashlight over every foot of terrain, and twisting his knee when he slipped on a patch of loose rock, Buck had limped home, more worried than ever. He'd kept his cell phone on but no one had called. And he still couldn't reach Terri.

He could remember feeling this helpless only one other time in his life—that was the day Steve had been struck by a sniper's bullet and carried back to camp to die in Buck's arms.

He'd just stepped onto the porch when he spotted the familiar headlights coming up the driveway. His pulse quickened. He'd know that old Jeep anywhere. He didn't know why she was here, but maybe Terri would have some idea where Quinn might be.

As the Jeep pulled up to the house and stopped, and he saw the small figure in the passenger seat, his heart contracted with a pain that was almost physical. Rushing down the steps, he flung the Jeep's door open, unhooked her seat belt and pulled his daughter into his arms.

"Thank God you're all right," he muttered, hugging her close.

She squirmed, pulling back a little. "I'm fine, Daddy. I was just at Terri's house."

Terri came around the back of the Jeep then, still wearing the clothes she'd worn on the river. She looked tired enough to drop.

"What happened?" Buck demanded before she could open her mouth. "I've been worried sick. I've got the sheriff and my security people combing the town for her. And I've been trying to reach you for the past couple of hours. Why in hell's name didn't you call me, Terri?"

She stopped in her tracks, looking as if he'd slapped her. "Call off the search," she said in a cold voice. "Then I'll explain—that is, if you're willing to listen."

He eased Quinn to the ground. "Go tell Mrs. Calloway you're here," he said. "Have her get you some supper if you're hungry. I'll be inside in a few minutes."

As his daughter dragged her feet into the house, Buck made a couple of quick calls on his phone, letting the searchers know his daughter was safe. Then, still shaken, he turned back to Terri.

"Well?"

She told him what had happened—the dead battery in her phone and her decision to take care of her grandmother's arrangements before going home. "I walked into the house to find that Quinn had broken in through the old pet door and fixed herself some cereal. She was asleep on the sofa. I couldn't call you, so I woke her up and drove her here. And now that she's home safe, I'll be going. Forgive me, Buck, I've had a long, rough day, and you aren't making it any easier."

Turning away, she started walking back around the Jeep.

"Wait!" Buck said.

"Yes?" She turned slowly back to face him, her gaze frigid.

"I need to know this. Did Quinn say anything about why she ran away?"

"Yes, she did. It was partly because she was bored. But mostly because she doesn't believe you love her. Quinn adores you, and she wants time with her father. But except for that first night, all you've done is go off to work and leave her with Mrs. Calloway. When you left for the river you didn't even tell her goodbye. If I was your daughter, Buck Morgan, I would run away, too—fast and far!"

Terri's words stung—mostly because they were true. It had taken this scare to make Buck realize how badly he'd neglected his precious little girl. "You're right, Terri. I'm sorry," he started to say, but she cut him off.

"Don't apologize to *me*!" she snapped. "And don't stop at just an apology to Quinn. Before you know it, she'll be a young woman. If she doesn't get the attention she needs from you, she'll look for it someplace else—and find it. By then it'll be too late. Think about that when you go back in the house and start planning your week."

Her lower lip quivered. She was getting emotional.

He hated it when women got emotional. "Why don't you come in and have some supper with us, Terri?" Buck said, hoping to calm her. "You must be hungry."

She shook her head. "I don't think that would be such a good idea."

"Then go on home and get some rest. Take a few days off for the funeral. Take a week, if you want. I can manage without my right-hand woman for a few days."

She sucked in her breath, looking as if she were about to explode. "You're going to have to manage a lot longer than that," she said. "Forget about the two weeks' notice I gave you. And forget about my doing the gala. I'm quitting as of right now."

Eight

Fighting tears, Terri drove down the canyon. She hadn't planned her farewell outburst. She'd wanted to leave Buck on friendly terms, not like this, in a storm of hurt and anger.

Should she apologize? Tell Buck she'd changed her mind and wanted more time to make plans? No, Terri told herself. What was done was done. The break she'd both needed and dreaded had been made. Why go back, and then have to do it again when the time came?

She'd meant to drive straight home. But her preoccupied mind hadn't been paying attention. By the time she realized where she was going, she was almost at the hotel complex that housed the Bucket List office. She slowed the Jeep, debating with herself. She was tired and she'd just made an emotional decision. She'd be wise to go home, get some rest and let things settle before taking action.

But why take the chance that she could go soft and change her mind? The office was empty now. She could let herself in, write up her resignation letter and leave it on Buck's desk. She could also go through her emails, deleting all but the most essential, and clean her personal items out of her desk. Buck would arrive in the morning to find her gone and everything in order.

She'd left the Jeep and was unlocking the office door when another wave of doubt overtook her. For the past ten years, her life had revolved around helping Buck run his business and his life. Now change was coming. She owed it to herself to let that change happen. She needed it to happen.

Still, letting go of everything familiar would be like closing her eyes and stepping off a precipice.

For almost half her life she'd been in love with Buck Morgan. She'd let her imagination build him into a romantic hero, excusing his faults and cleaning up after his mistakes. But tonight had opened her eyes and slammed her against the hard wall of reality. The man was an insensitive jerk with skewed priorities. The people who cared most about him—especially Quinn—were the ones he took most for granted. No wonder he'd never remarried after Diane. And no wonder his daughter had left the house this afternoon.

Walk away, she told herself as she turned the key

in the lock. *Now, while the door's open, walk away and don't look back.*

It took her fifteen minutes to bring up her computer, compose a brief, impersonal letter of resignation and send it to the printer. It took another fifteen minutes to clean out her inbox and shut down her computer, collect a few personal items in a cardboard box, sign the letter, and leave it on Buck's desk, where he'd see it first thing tomorrow.

After securing Buck's door, she picked up the cardboard box, locked the outer office and walked to her Jeep. She'd put out some feelers a few days ago and already had a couple of job offers. After her grandmother was buried, she would make a final decision and start packing.

She was done here—finished with the job and the man. It was time to begin a new chapter in her life.

Buck arrived at work an hour early. With Terri on funeral leave—he refused to believe she'd really meant what she'd said about quitting—and with a four-day accumulation of phone messages and email to answer, the day was bound to be a busy one.

Parking the Hummer in its reserved spot, he whistled on his way to the outside door of his private office. He'd promised to take Quinn horseback riding after work. She'd given him a scare last night, but he didn't have the heart to punish her. He would show her a good time, they would forgive each other and all would be well in his world.

Stepping into the office, the first thing he noticed was the sheet of paper in the exact center of his desk. He picked it up. He read it. He swore out loud.

He read it again—the tersely worded letter of resignation, so cold, so formal. His jaw tightened. Maybe, just maybe, there was a way to end this nonsense. Striding into Terri's office, he opened the filing cabinet that held the personnel records for his employees. Since Terri had arranged the file folders in alphabetical order, finding the one he needed was easy. He took a quick look inside to make sure the folder contained what he needed. Then, clutching it in his hand, he locked the office, climbed into the Hummer and roared out of the parking lot.

Terri had returned home last night, taken a long, sudsy shower, pulled on an oversize cotton T-shirt and burrowed into bed. The next thing she knew, it was morning, and someone—or something—was pounding on her front door.

Throwing on the old blue terry cloth robe that had been Steve's, she stumbled across the living room to the door. A look though the tiny glass peephole was enough to make her wish she'd stayed in bed.

"Go away," she said loudly enough to be heard through the door. "I'm sleeping."

"I'm not going anywhere, Terri. Let me in." He sounded mad enough to kick the door down. Unhooking the chain and sliding back the bolt, she opened the door a few inches.

"Can't this wait?" she asked. "You just woke me out of the first decent sleep I've had in days."

"No, it can't wait, and I'm not leaving. So unless you want me to stand here and yell at you, you might as well let me in."

She opened the door. Spotlessly groomed and ready for the day, he stepped across the threshold like a conqueror taking possession. He'd spent a lot of time in this house when he and Steve were boys. But after his deployment, Terri couldn't remember his ever coming to visit. Had he stayed away because it held too many painful memories, or because he just never thought of it?

He glanced around the room, maybe thinking how little the place had changed. Terri noticed the personnel folder in his hand. It would be hers, of course. She should have realized this would happen. Too bad she wasn't better prepared.

He motioned toward the couch, his expression a thundercloud. "Sit down," he said. "I want to show you something."

He wasn't her boss anymore, Terri reminded herself. She didn't have to take his orders. But it wasn't worth arguing the point. She sat. He took a seat beside her, opened the folder and took out a one-page document with the Bucket List letterhead at the top.

"This is the employment contract you signed when you went to work for me," he said. "Read it. Pay special attention to paragraph three."

Terri sighed. She'd been over that document with

every new hire at Bucket List. "I don't need to read it," she said. "I know what it says."

"Then you know you're *required* to give two weeks' notice."

"I did!"

"Not officially, in writing—not until last night."

"You're actually going to hold me to that?"

"You're damned right I am—even it means suing you for breach of contract."

Terri's jaw dropped. "You wouldn't dare!"

One dark eyebrow slithered upward. "Wouldn't I? Just try me, lady."

They glared at each other like two fighters going toe-to-toe. Then, abruptly, Buck exhaled and shook his head. "If you want to go, I won't stop you, Terri. But does it have to be like this, completely gone overnight, right in the heart of our busiest season? Damn it, don't you understand? I *need* you!"

If he'd raged and threatened all morning, nothing could've had as much effect as those last three words. The only times Terri had heard them before was in connection with an order, as in *I need you to requisition more coffee.*

Unattached to anything else, the words struck Terri like a knife to the heart. But they didn't mean what she wanted them to mean, she told herself. All he really needed was her help at work.

"Two more weeks—just until the gala's over, that's all I'm asking," he said. "Give me that, and I'll give

you a severance package to make your head spin—
and I'll write a great recommendation to go with it."

"And if I leave now? If I don't come back at all?"

His mouth hardened. "I won't take you to court—
it would be bad publicity for the company. But you
walk away with nothing. Your choice."

Terri broke eye contact and gazed down at her
hands. The reality was, the transition to a new job and
the move to a new place would take time and money.
Her grandmother's care had taken most of her savings.
The funeral service would take the rest. The extra two
weeks of work and the severance package Buck had
promised could make all the difference for her. Pride
had its price, and right now she couldn't afford it.

"When's your grandmother's service going to be?"
He spoke as if he already knew he'd beaten her.

"Tomorrow—at the graveside. Just a simple cer-
emony. She had no living relatives except me, and
most of her old friends are already gone." She met his
cool gaze. "There's no reason I can't be back at work
the next day. There'll be a lot to do before the gala."
She gave him a steely look. "But since you brought
up the subject of contracts, Buck, I want my severance terms in writing."

A look of surprise flashed across his face. Rising,
he hid it quickly. "Fine. I'll write up an acceptance of
your resignation and the terms of your severance and
have it on your desk when you come in." He sounded
like a stranger, this man she'd known since his boy-

hood. But that was how things would have to be from here on out.

He walked to the door, then paused. "I'm sorry about your grandmother, Terri. She was a fine lady, and she was very good to me." The door closed behind him. Seconds later Terri heard the sound of the Hummer starting up. The old Buck would have put his arms around her and given her a brotherly hug. But things had changed between them, perhaps forever.

Feeling as if he'd just been kicked by a mule, Buck drove back to the office. He'd gotten what he wanted—Terri's services for another two weeks. But the outcome of their meeting didn't feel like a victory. He could have told her how much he valued and appreciated her. Instead he'd bullied and threatened her into their agreement. He didn't like himself much right now. As Terri's late grandmother might have put it, he felt lower than a snake's belly.

When Terri came back, he would treat her right—give her the generous severance she deserved and write her a recommendation fit to win her the Nobel Prize for administrative assistants, if there was such a thing. And for the next two weeks he would be the very soul of kindness and respect. But after last night, Buck knew better than to think he could change her mind through any action on his part. And if he kept trying to manipulate her, he'd just drive her further away. Terri wanted more from life than what she'd found here in Porter Hollow. If he cared about her happiness he would ease the way for her to go.

But what was he going to do after she was gone?

Pulling into the parking lot behind the hotel, he groaned. The big white Lincoln that Diane kept in a garage at the airstrip for her visits was parked outside his private office. Whatever had motivated his ex-wife to come all the way here, it couldn't be good.

For a moment he was tempted to turn around and leave. But no, better to get it over with, he told himself. The sooner he faced her the sooner he could finish their business and get on with the rest of his day.

Using the outside door, he walked into his office. Diane, immaculate in a white linen suit with a two-thousand-dollar designer scarf at her throat, was leaning back in his leather chair with her gold metallic Jimmy Choo sandals resting on his desktop. Her platinum hair curled softly around her face. She was showgirl tall, a woman who would have turned heads even without the surgical enhancements to her face and body.

"Hello, Buck." Her voice sounded like the growl of a tigress getting ready to pounce.

Buck remained on his feet. "This is a surprise. You could've called and let me know you were coming."

"Why should I? As part owner of this company, there's no reason I can't show up anytime I want."

"Can I order you anything, an iced tea, maybe?"

"Don't bother. This won't take long." She swung her feet to the floor and sat up. "I thought I should tell you before I went to your house. I'm here to take Quinn home."

That got his attention. "No!" He clenched his fist as her words sank in. "She's here for the summer. We have a legal agreement that says so." Even as he spoke, Buck remembered the email on Quinn's computer, telling her mother how miserable she was. Lord, how was Diane going to twist this against him?

"Legal agreements can be changed. You went off and left Quinn with the nanny for four days without even telling her goodbye. She was so unhappy that she ran away and was lost for hours."

"Who told you that?"

"Mrs. Calloway. She called me last night—said she had the child's best interest at heart."

Buck felt as if the cold jaws of a trap were closing around him—a trap he'd walked into blindly. He adored his daughter. It wasn't as if he'd wanted to leave her. But he simply hadn't paid enough attention to her needs. He'd made sure she'd be taken care of, and yet he hadn't bothered to do anything to make her *happy*. He'd set himself up for this, and now he was vulnerable. "It was an emergency," he said, realizing as he spoke how lame the excuse sounded.

"Yes, I understand." Her voice dripped sarcasm. "A business emergency. I've already called my lawyer to discuss suing for full custody, on the grounds that your work makes you unfit to be a father. He thinks we have a good chance of winning."

Buck fought down a surge of rage and panic. Leaving Quinn had been a bad decision. But he realized that now and had already resolved to change his behavior going forward. And anyway, she'd been safe and well cared for the whole time. Surely he didn't deserve to lose her for that.

"Even you wouldn't be that cruel," he said. "You know Quinn means the world to me."

"Does she?" Diane laughed. "You couldn't prove that by me, Buck."

He caught the glint of triumph in her jade-green eyes. She'd backed him into a corner, and she knew it. But something told Buck she hadn't chartered a flight and walked in here dressed to kill out of concern for Quinn. Yes, she loved her daughter—but if she truly wanted to take Quinn away from him, she'd have gone straight to his house, not to the office. Somehow, there was a business angle to this. One thing he'd learned during their brief marriage was that Diane was a master manipulator.

Eyes narrowing, he studied her. "What is it you really want, Diane?"

A smile curved her silicone-plumped lips. "That, my dear, depends on what *you* want. Maybe we can strike an agreement."

"I'll tell you what I want," Buck said. "I want you to leave Quinn here and forget this nonsense about suing for custody. You don't even want her full-time. Summers, when she's here with me, you're as free as a bird. You like it that way."

"Perhaps. But if it's in Quinn's best interest to be

with me full-time…" She left the words dangling, the threat implied.

Buck struggled to cool his temper, knowing that if he exploded, the standoff would be lost. "All right," he said. "Tell me what it would take for you to back off."

Her calculating expression didn't change. "Another thousand a month in alimony might make a difference. Along with an additional two percent of the company."

Buck exhaled in disgust, knowing she'd planned this all along, and that short of giving up his daughter or going through months of legal wrangling, there was little he could do other than concede. "What the hell," he growled. "However it's split up, it'll all go to Quinn after we're gone. I'll have the papers drawn up."

"Don't bother." She unzipped her briefcase. "I have them right here. All you need to do is sign."

"You're unbelievable."

"I know." She smiled and held out a pen. Buck bent over the desk, scanned the document to make sure it held no surprises and scrawled his name. He could try to bargain her down to less, or even fight this in court if he had to, but right now all he wanted was to have her leave—without taking Quinn.

"I'll have Bob witness my signature and make a copy when he comes in, which should be any minute," he said.

"Where's Terri? Doesn't she usually handle that sort of thing?"

"Her grandmother passed away. The funeral's to-morrow."

Diane shrugged. "I suppose you can always fill her in later. She'll make sure the paperwork goes where it should. You wouldn't really trust Bob with it, surely?"

"I'm going to have to," Buck admitted through gritted teeth. "Terri will be back after the funeral, but she's put in her notice."

"Terri's leaving?" Diane's laugh was a derisive snort. "I can't even imagine that, after the way she's always mooned after you. Maybe she's finally come to her senses and realized she wasn't your type."

"What are you talking about?" Buck stared at his ex as if she'd just doused him with cold water.

Diane laughed again. "Are you blind? Don't you know the poor thing's been in love with you for years? Even when you and I were married, I could see it in the way she looked at you. I'm just surprised you haven't taken advantage and given her the thrill of a roll between the sheets." She cocked her head, gazing at him like a curious bird. "Good Lord, you haven't, have you?"

Heat flooded Buck's face. He turned away, hoping she wouldn't see the rush of color.

"Well, have you? Have you slept with that poor little plain Jane?"

Buck was tempted to put Diane and her superficial assumptions in her place. But telling her the truth would just open himself and Terri up to more ridicule. But really, Terri, a plain Jane? Not hardly.

Buck was saved from a lie by the sounds of Bob and the temps arriving for work. He opened the in-

side door of his office and called the young man inside to witness his signature and take the document
to the copy machine.

"I'll be taking Quinn out for brunch before I leave,"
Diane was saying. "And maybe I'll fly in again for
the gala. I'd love the chance to dress up and mingle.
How would you like to be my escort?"

Buck stood in the doorway, waiting for Bob to return with the copy. "Sorry," he said, glancing back at
her. "I already have a date."

"Oh, really?" Her eyes widened. "Who?"

Buck thought fast. "Terri."

Harriet Cooper's graveside funeral was sparsely
attended. At ninety-one, the old woman had outlived
most of her friends and family. Terri was there, of
course, in a simple black knit dress and a black straw
hat with a ribbon that fluttered down her slender back.
Also in attendance were a couple of people from Canyon Shadows, the funeral director and the pastor of
her church, who gave a eulogy and led the prayer.

Buck, who'd taken the chance and sent a spray of
pink roses for the casket, had brought Quinn to the
service. Since he'd dismissed Mrs. Calloway the day
before and was wary of hiring anyone new who might
also report back to Diane, he'd had little choice except
to keep his daughter with him. Quinn, who'd never
been to a funeral, had been curious enough to come
along. Besides, she'd wanted to be there for Terri.
Looking fresh and pretty in her white sundress, she'd

stood quietly while the casket was lowered into the grave. She was bound to have questions later. Maybe they could have a good talk over lunch.

During the eulogy, Buck's gaze was drawn again and again to Terri. She stood at the graveside, hands clasped in front of her, eyes masked by her sunglasses. She looked tired and fragile, but all the same, he was struck by her beauty—a beauty of strength and integrity that went bone deep.

Are you blind? Don't you know the poor thing's been in love with you for years?

Diane's cutting words came back to him as he studied the woman who'd been at his side for more than a decade. Was that why she'd allowed herself to be lured into his bed—because she loved him?

Knowing Terri as he did, it was the only reason that made sense. Not that it could be allowed to make a difference. Whatever her feelings for him—and his for her—the past was unchangeable. Too much water under the bridge, as Harriet would have put it.

The service had ended. Terri walked toward her Jeep, then, as if remembering her manners, turned and came back toward Buck and Quinn. Buck hadn't spoken to her since their awkward parting at her house. Maybe it was time for some fence-mending. And maybe he really *should* invite her to the gala as his date. In the past she'd always worked the gala behind the scenes, making sure everything ran smoothly. This year, her last time, she deserved to put on a pretty gown and enjoy herself. Getting her to say yes might take some persuasion. But at least having Quinn here should make the asking easier.

"Thank you both for coming." She was polite, if cool. "And thank you for the flowers, Buck. You didn't have to do that, but I know grandma would have loved them. Pink roses were her favorite." Looking down at Quinn, she smiled. "You look so pretty, Quinn. Would you like a rose to keep for yourself?"

Quinn hesitated, as if thinking. "Thanks. But could I take two? I know what I want to do with them."

At Terri's nod, Quinn walked back to the grave and slipped two long-stemmed pink roses from the spray of flowers. As Buck and Terri watched, she carried them down the row of graves, paused and laid one rose next to Buck's mother's headstone. Then, crossing to the next row, she laid the other at the base of Steve's.

Buck could almost feel his heart being crushed. Terri's breath caught. Her fingers crept into his hand. He clasped them tightly as the memories slammed into him—his mother watching him walk away for the last time, and Steve, wounded and bleeding in his arms, the light fading from his eyes.

I'm sorry, Mom. And I'm sorry, Steve. Oh, God, so sorry. That should be my grave, not yours, Steve, your child, not mine. If only I could take your place now, like you took mine back then...

Before Buck could continue the thought, Quinn came dancing back to him, a smile on her face.

"That was a lovely thing to do, Quinn," Terri said, and pulled her hand away from Buck's. "Thank you

for remembering my brother today—and your grandmother, too."

"Daddy told me Steve was his best friend," Quinn
said.

"That's right." Biting back his emotion, Buck laid
a hand on her small, suntanned shoulder and changed
the subject. "Quinn and I were about to go to lunch
at the Ledges. Why don't you come with us, Terri?"

He sensed a flicker in her eyes. He'd been pretty
hard on her yesterday. He wouldn't blame her if she
said no.

"Please come with us, Terri," Quinn begged, tugging at her hand. "It'll be lots more fun with you
there!"

Quinn could be irresistible when she wanted something. Right now, Buck was grateful for it. Terri gave
in with a smile. "All right. Come to think of it, I'm
pretty hungry—starving, actually."

The Ledges was an upscale restaurant on the road
out of town. Its floor-to-ceiling windows, as well as an
outside deck, let customers enjoy a stunning panorama
of towering red-and-white sandstone cliffs while they
dined on organic gourmet meals. Since Buck was part
owner of the place, he and his guests could expect
VIP treatment.

Terri scanned the lunch menu, pondering the soup-
and-salad combos. Beside her, Quinn was chattering
nonstop.

"Now that Mrs. C. is gone, Daddy says that if I behave I can come to work with him and help out—run errands, keep the break room neat, stuff like that. It'll be like having a real job. Maybe I'll even get paid." She cast a plaintive look at her father.

"That's open to negotiation," Buck replied with a mock scowl.

"I can help you, too, Terri," she said. "Daddy always says you're his right-hand woman. Maybe I can be his right-hand girl."

"That sounds like a fine idea," Terri said, thinking Buck must not have told his daughter she was leaving in two weeks. How her going would affect Quinn would be one more issue to deal with—and a reason to be glad she hadn't just walked away.

The server took their orders and brought their drinks. Sitting across from Terri, Buck took a sip from his glass, then cleared his throat. "Terri, I brought you here with an ulterior motive," he said. "I have a favor to ask, and I hope you'll say yes."

Terri's instincts prickled. "That depends on what it is."

"It's about the gala," he said. "Every year you've worked behind the scenes and done a terrific job. This year I'd like you to come out front and cohost the event with me."

Terri's first reaction was a mild panic. She had her share of experience mixing with wealthy politicians and celebrities when they came to the resort as guests. But her role as part of the staff always provided a bit of a barrier. Cohosting the gala, that barrier would be gone. What if she made a fool of herself? She scrambled for excuses.

"Have you thought this through, Buck? How can I do my job if I'm out front socializing?"

"Bob can manage things if you show him what to do. You'll have two weeks to train him."

Terri shook her head. "I don't know if he can do it. Besides, I don't have anything to wear."

"That's an easy fix," Buck said. "Buy yourself an outfit. Charge it to the company. It's a legitimate work expense."

Quinn had been all ears. "Take me shopping with you, Terri! I'll help you pick out a dress! You'll be like Cinderella at the ball!"

Two against one. Terri could feel herself folding. "I still don't think it's a good idea," she said to Buck.

"You'll do fine. Now stop worrying and eat your salad." His eyes twinkled. "That's an order."

Nine

With three days to go, Terri's plans for the Seventh Annual Bucket List Gala were falling into place. The hotel's convention facilities included a large elegant ballroom where the party would be held. The restaurant staff would provide the food and drinks, an updated version of the customary gala menu that would include a few surprises. The music and entertainment had been booked more than a year in advance, the RSVP invitations mailed out six weeks earlier.

Bob had been carefully trained to coordinate everything behind the scenes. It would be a huge responsibility. Terri was already running him through his paces like an army drill sergeant. The young man was bright and capable when he put his mind to the task. She only hoped she could trust him to stay focused and do his best.

Between the gala preparations and her regular office duties, Terri had scarcely thought of the one urgent task that remained—shopping for a gown.

It was Quinn who reminded her. "We can go today after work," Buck's daughter said, taking charge. "Can I invite Ann Marie to come with us?"

"Sure. We'll make a party of it. Ice cream for all when we're done," Terri said. Ann Marie, Evie Redfeather's nine-year-old grandniece, was visiting for the summer. She and Quinn had become fast friends. They'd be having a sleepover at Evie's the night of the gala.

When Buck heard about the plan he insisted that they leave work an hour early. They picked up Ann Marie at Evie's and headed for the outlet mall where Terri had taken Quinn earlier to buy clothes. Buck had given her carte blanche on choosing a gown, but Terri was too practical to spend a lot of money on a dress she'd wear only once. At the mall there was a discount shop that sold bridal and formal wear. With luck, it wouldn't take too long to find something suitable.

But she hadn't counted on trying to please two little fashionistas. Quinn and Ann Marie, seated on folding chairs, insisted that Terri try on and model every gown in her size.

They shook their heads when she walked out in a plain, modest black sheath that Terri might have bought if she'd been there alone. And they hooted with laughter when she showed off a purple bridesmaid dress with big puffy sleeves, followed by a strapless, ruffled pink prom gown. The next dress wasn't bad style-wise, but the lime-green color made her look ill. By the end of an entertaining hour, all three had to admit there wasn't a wearable gown in the place. Now what?

"I know," Quinn said. "There's a boutique in town where my mom likes to shop. Let's look there."

Terri suppressed a groan. She wasn't keen on anything that might look like Diane, and she could just imagine what a dress from that place might cost. But with two pairs of small hands tugging her toward the Jeep, she gave in.

Most of the gowns at the boutique, though beautiful, were too flashy for Terri's taste. But when she tried on a simple, soft teal silk that draped her body like mist, her two little critics jumped up and cheered. She'd found her perfect dress. But when she checked the price, she almost fainted. It was the most expensive gown in the exclusive shop.

She was handing it back to the saleslady to put away when Quinn gave her ribs a none-too-gentle nudge. "Go for it, Terri!" she ordered. "Daddy said you could buy anything you wanted on the company credit card. Besides, you've earned this."

Absolved of guilt, Terri reached into her purse and pulled out the plastic. She had a pair of dangly gold earrings at home that would look fine for the night. And although the dress begged for new gold sandals, she knew she'd be on her feet a lot. Covered by the long skirt, her comfy black pumps would barely show.

Terri paid for the dress and came back to find the girls whispering together. "We want to do your hair for the party," Quinn announced. "Come to Ann Marie's before you get dressed. Don't worry. We're *really* good!"

Terri had planned on going to the hotel beauty shop, or even just washing her hair and letting it hang loose. But the two little girls looked so eager and excited to play fairy godmother. What could it hurt? Why not let them have fun?

"Sure," she said. "Now let's go get ice cream."

After dropping both girls off at Evie's, Terri drove home. The day had been a long one, and for some reason, trying on all those gowns had left her exhausted. All she wanted was to curl up on the bed and go to sleep. But she still had things to do, and resting now would only keep her awake at night.

Entering the spare bedroom she'd converted to an office, she switched on her computer. Bringing up her email, she scanned the messages—mostly junk, but one jumped out at her. The managers of a big ski resort in Park City wanted to hire her. Since they needed someone right away, they wanted her to come and make arrangements at the earliest possible date.

The drive to Park City and back could be made in one very long day, or two shorter days. But there was no way she could go before the gala. She composed a reply to the message, suggesting a time early next week. It would be an ideal situation for her. Park City was a fair-sized town in a picturesque setting, with year-round social and cultural activities. She'd never skied, but she could learn.

She clicked the send button and put the computer in sleep mode. She really should finish checking her emails. But she was worn out tonight. The idea of getting into her pajamas, washing her face, brushing her teeth and watching a couple hours of mindless TV sounded like just what she needed.

Barefoot and dressed in her sweats, she pattered into the bathroom, wiped off the little makeup she wore and reached for her toothbrush. She'd thrown away the crumpled, empty toothpaste tube that morning, but she'd bought a fresh tube a couple of weeks ago and put it in the bathroom closet.

Opening the closet door, she scanned the shelves. There was the toothpaste, right next to…

Her heart dropped as her eyes fixed on the unopened box of tampons—the box she'd bought the same time as the toothpaste and expected to have needed before now. She'd never been 100 percent regular, but unless her calculations were off, her period was almost ten days overdue.

Lord have mercy, could she be pregnant with Buck's baby?

It was stress, that was all, Terri told herself as she drove to work the next day. Between the river trip, losing her grandmother, the upcoming gala and the un-settling situation at work, she was a bundle of nerves. The anxiety could have delayed her period. That, or she'd just lost track of the days and her count was off.

If she had serious concerns, she could always buy a home pregnancy test. But surely it was too soon for that. Any day now, her period would start, and she'd know she'd been worried for nothing. Meanwhile, if she could, she'd put it out of her mind. She was deal-ing with enough right now.

She'd arrived ahead of the staff, but the inside door to Buck's office was standing open. As she walked past, he stood, walked around his desk and motioned her inside.

"Have a seat, Terri. The restaurant just brought coffee. Let me pour you a cup." He picked up an in-sulated carafe from the silver tray on the credenza. "Cream with no sugar, right?"

"You should know by now." Terri settled into a chair facing the desk and took the steaming porcelain mug he offered her. The coffee was hot and good, but it failed to warm the cold spot in the pit of her stom-ach. In a few days' time, this job and this man would be part of her past. She should be excited at the pros-pect of a new life. But right now the thought of not seeing him every workday, perhaps not seeing him ever again, made her feel as if she was lost without a compass.

One decision had been made in the dark of last night. If she really did turn out to be pregnant—which she almost certainly wasn't—she would leave town without telling him. She'd had a front-row seat for his miserable shotgun marriage to Diane—and she'd seen how the woman continued to manipulate him, using Quinn. For Buck to marry yet another woman out of duty to his child, a woman he didn't love, would be unthinkable, both for her and for him.

Buck sat down again. "You look a little frayed. Is everything all right?"

"Fine," she lied.

"How are plans for the gala going? Quinn told me you finally bought a dress."

"Yes, I did. It's beautiful. And I've agreed to let Quinn and Ann Marie do my hair."

"You're one brave lady." A smile lit his sky-blue eyes and deepened the dimple in his cheek. If she really was pregnant, her baby had won the gene pool lottery, Terri mused, then quickly banished the thought.

"They were so excited about helping me get ready, I couldn't refuse," she said. "If my hair looks a little strange, I'll just call it a fashion statement."

"If you don't like it, you can always take it down before the gala."

"No way. I'll wear it proudly."

His gaze warmed. "I can't imagine any other woman doing that," he said. "You're amazing."

He was getting to her. Terri squelched a rush of emotion. "Have you told Quinn I'm leaving?" she asked, changing the subject.

"I thought I'd let you do that."

Coward, she thought, then spoke. "Quinn might take it hard. I've always been here for her. I can tell her, but you'll want to give her some extra TLC just to make sure she's all right."

"We could always have a farewell dinner before you go, just the three of us," Buck said.

"I may not have time for that." She told him about the job offer in Park City. "They want somebody right away. If I decide to take it, I'll barely have time to pack my things and put the house on the market."

"So soon?" He looked stunned. "I'll give you a great recommendation if they ask, of course. But it's still sinking in that you're really doing this."

"For me, too," Terri said, then rose before he could strip away her fragile self-control. "I think I just heard Bob come in. Time for me to crack the whip."

Buck watched her walk out of his office, painfully aware that soon she would walk out of his life. Lord, what would he do without her? How would it feel the first time he came into work and it hit him that she was really gone?

In so many ways, Terri was irreplaceable. Where else would he find a woman who looked spectacular coated with river mud, a woman who could navigate a rapid, pack a parachute, skydive out of a plane and guide novice hikers through a slot canyon—a woman who would trust two little girls to fix her hair for a formal event where she'd want to look her best?

And what other woman would wake him out of a

drug-fogged sleep with loving as tender and passionate as any he'd ever known? He would never forget
the morning Terri had stolen into his bed. But he was
less sure how and when she'd also crept into his heart.

Buck backed his black Jaguar out of the garage and
drove down the canyon to pick up Terri for the gala.
It was raining—not a cloudburst but a fine mist that
cooled the summer darkness and softened the lights
along Main Street. In this desert country, rain was always welcome, even on the night of the biggest charity event of the year.

Terri had insisted that this was work, not a date.
So why did Buck feel like a high school boy on prom
night as he rang her doorbell and waited on the covered stoop for her to answer? He'd driven himself
a little crazy trying to imagine Terri in an evening
gown. In the years he'd known her, she'd worn mostly
jeans or school clothes, or her khaki work uniform.
Even the black dress she'd worn to her grandmother's
funeral had been little more than a long T-shirt with
a belt. But she was a beautiful woman. In the right
dress she would look stunning.

He rang the doorbell again. There was a rustle of
movement on the other side; then the door opened.
Terri stood before him wearing a black nylon rain
poncho with the hood covering her hair. He exhaled
in disappointment. The unveiling would have to wait.

"Sorry the yard's such a muddy mess," she apologized. "You could've stayed in the car, honked me out and saved your shoes."

"I've never honked a girl out in my life," Buck said. "And I never will. You deserve better than that."

"An old-fashioned gentleman! Who'd have thought?" She flashed him a dazzling smile as she locked the door. "You look smashing in that tux, by the way."

"I'll return the compliment when I can see more of you." He ushered her into the Jag, closed the door and went around to the driver's seat. "We should get there just in time to check everything over before the guests start arriving."

She snuggled into the soft leather seat. "I just hope Bob will be all right. Otherwise, I'll have to take over and help him."

"Don't even think about it. He'll do fine. Your job tonight is to charm our guests and talk them into extra digits on their donation checks." Closing the door he gave her a sidelong glance. All he could see was the hood of her poncho and the tip of her nose just visible past the edge. "It isn't raining in the car," he said, hoping she'd take the hint.

"But it might be raining when we get to the hotel." Was she teasing him? If so, it was working. He was wild to see her out of that blasted poncho. He only hoped he could keep his hands off her.

They pulled up to the hotel's covered main entrance, where a valet was waiting to take the car and park it. Buck took Terri's hand to help her out of the car. The light grip of her fingers recalled that moment after the funeral when Quinn had placed a rose on Steve's grave. He remembered how Terri's fingers had crept into his palm, so trusting, as if seeking comfort. How he'd wanted to give her that comfort and more. But he couldn't have done that without lying to her.

He wanted this woman, damn it—wanted her in his bed and in his life. But it was useless to hope. She was already moving on, and the tragic truth he'd be honor-bound to share before he could even attempt a real relationship with her would destroy any chance of lasting happiness.

Still covered in her poncho, she crossed the hotel lobby with him. The coat check window was next to the ballroom entrance. Buck paused, turned to face her and, without a word, unfastened the snap at her throat and swept the poncho off her shoulders.

She took his breath away.

The sleeveless gown was simple perfection. The silk fabric was draped to follow the curves of her glorious body, allowing an ample glimpse of cleavage at the bodice, then clinging downward to a point above her knees, where it flared into a softly flowing skirt. Mermaid style, Diane would have called it, if Buck remembered right.

Terri wore no jewelry except a pair of shoulder-skimming golden earrings—probably not even real gold, but they were enough. Her sun-burnished skin, glowing against the deep teal silk, was all the dazzle she needed.

Her hair—he might have chosen to see it loose and

flowing, but he had to admit her young stylists had done an impressive job. French braids swept her long chestnut locks back from the sides of her face to join at the nape of her neck in a single loose braid woven with strands of thin gold ribbon.

"What do you think?" She looked at him, so adorably self-conscious that Buck wanted to sweep her into his arms and show her the effect she was really having on him.

He found his voice. "You look amazing. My compliments to your hairdressers."

"They did all right, didn't they? And they had so much fun." She glanced at her wrist before she realized she wasn't wearing a watch. "Let's get busy. The doors will be opening soon."

Even looking like a goddess, she was all business. Buck trailed her through the back rooms, where she spoke with the serving, security and electrical crews, then touched base with Bob and went over his checklist.

"Wow, you look great!" the young man said.

She gave him a self-effacing smile. "Thanks, but it's just work, Bob. Everything you've done looks good, but in case you need me, I'll be right out front."

"Don't worry, he'll manage fine, Terri." Buck pulled her back down the hall toward the ballroom. "Now stop fussing and breathe. Yes, you've got a job to do, but this is your last gala. I want you to have a good time tonight."

"Is that an order, boss?"

"Absolutely." He linked his arm through hers and

led her into the empty ballroom. Everything here was
in readiness. The oak floor was polished to a golden
gleam. The three immense crystal chandeliers blazed
with light. The tables that ringed the dance floor were
set with candles, crystal and silver, the buffet tables
and the long antique bar at the far end fully stocked
and ready.

The quartet of jazz musicians, who traveled with
the legendary singer Terri had been lucky enough to
book, were just warming up. Little riffs floated off
the keys of the grand piano. Soft blues notes rose from
the saxophone, trumpet and bass. The players in this
jazz ensemble were among the best in the world. It
had cost a small fortune to bring them here, fresh
from a major gig in Las Vegas. But nothing was too
good for the gala.

Buck could sense the tension that radiated from
Terri's body as she mentally micromanaged everything. *Let it go*, he wanted to tell her. *With you on my
arm, I'll be the envy of every man in the ballroom.
Just relax and let me show you off.*

Struck by a sudden inspiration, he turned her toward him. "Stay right here," he said. "Don't move an
inch till I get back." He strode across the floor to where
the band was ending its warm-up. Stepping in close,
he introduced himself and asked for a special favor.

The four musicians grinned and nodded. "Anything
for the lady," the piano player said.

The music started as Buck walked back to where
Terri waited. The intro began on the tinkling piano,

then the bass started throbbing a sensual underbeat. The trumpet and saxophone took up the mellow strains of "At Last," and Buck faced Terri and held out his hand. "Dance with me," he said.

Her lips parted, but she didn't speak as he drew her into his arms. She was a little stiff and self-conscious at first, but as he pulled her close enough to be guided by his body, she softened against him, slipping into the beat of the music.

Her satiny cheek rested against his. He breathed her in, filling his senses with her sexy-clean, womanly aroma. Her curves skimmed his body, the contact hardening his arousal. There was no way she couldn't be feeling it. But she didn't pull away. He'd made love to this woman, Buck reminded himself. He'd been inside her—and damn it all, he ached to be there again. But that was the least of what he was feeling now. How could he let her go after tonight? How could he watch her walk away, knowing that even if he saw her again, she would no longer be part of his life?

She tilted her head to smile up at him. "I feel like Cinderella at the ball," she whispered.

Buck's arm tightened around her waist, pulling her closer. It would be heaven to hold her like this forever, he thought. But he was no prince. And like in the fairy tale, the enchantment would be fated to end when the ball was over.

Terri closed her eyes, savoring these last few moments in Buck's arms. Soon the song would end. Soon the doors to the ballroom would open and the streams of glittering guests would begin flowing in. In the hours ahead it would be her job to make sure everyone was welcomed, and to talk up the children's clinics, homeless shelters and other charities the gala supported. Tomorrow she would pack for the drive to Park City and organize the house for a possible move. But now, for this brief flicker of time, she was in his arms, and he was hers. Until the music ended and the ballroom doors opened to let in the guests, nothing else mattered.

The event started promptly at eight o'clock and ran smoothly from beginning to end. For Terri, the hours passed in a blur of greeting guests that included the governor and state officials, business and community leaders, TV and movie personalities, and a host of other wealthy donors As the party continued, she'd left Buck's side over and over again to work the floor, making sure everyone felt at home and had what they needed—a drink, a pen, directions to the restroom or a good seat for the entertainment. She'd seen enough galas to know what had to be done.

By the time the crowd was thinning out, Terri's smile felt pasted on. Her feet had gone numb, and she was so tired she could barely stand. As the last guests trickled out the door, she made her way to Buck's side. He gave her a smile, looking as fresh and energetic as when he'd walked in.

"Sit down," he said. "You look ready to drop."

"I am." She sank onto a handy chair. "Will we need to stay for the cleanup?"

"No, Bob can make sure everything's shipshape. He's done a good job tonight. Remind me to give him a raise on Monday." His expression froze as his eyes met Terri's. She could guess what he was thinking. She wouldn't be around to remind him of *anything* on Monday. She would be gone.

"Come on, we don't need to stay." He extended his hand to help her up. A word from him summoned an attendant with her poncho. He laid it gently over her shoulders as they walked out a side entrance. The black Jaguar waited in the shadows, where he must have told the valet to leave it.

"You were wonderful tonight," he said as he opened the door for her. "Thank you."

"I was just doing my job." She settled into the cushiony leather seat as he walked around the car and climbed in on the driver's side. Terri steeled herself for the drive home and what could be their final goodbye. Whatever happened, she told herself, she would not cry until he was gone.

"Your job? Was that all it was?" He touched her shoulder. "Look at me, Terri."

Despite her resolve, the tears were already welling—tears that refused to hide as she turned to face him. His cupped hand lifted her chin as he leaned in to kiss her, gently at first, then, in a release of passion that was like the bursting of a dam, he crushed her close, his mouth possessing her, stirring deep urges that were too strong to resist.

"Come home with me, Terri." His voice was a rough whisper. His lips skimmed hers as he spoke. "Come just for tonight. Let me make love to you."

Terri struggled to speak, then realized there was nothing to say. She wanted what he wanted, and he would know it without a word.

Ten

Rain drummed on the roof of the Jaguar, trickling in silver streams down the side windows as the sleek black car wound its way up the canyon. Terri sat in trembling silence, stealing glances at Buck's chiseled profile. Her pulse skittered as she remembered his words.

Come just for tonight. Let me make love to you.

At least he wasn't playing games. He'd stated his intentions and made it clear that there wouldn't be another time after this. Delicious sex with no strings attached. Wasn't that what they both wanted? After so many years together, wasn't it as good a way as any to say goodbye?

He pulled through the gate and up the driveway. A touch on the remote opened the garage. He pulled inside and closed the door behind them. From there, they entered through a door into the back hallway off the kitchen. Terri knew Buck's house well. But she'd never been here in the middle of the night, on her way to the man's bed.

She'd expected him to lead her to the stairs, but they were still in the hallway when he stopped, stripped off her poncho and pulled her to him. His kiss was pure seduction, slow, languorous and deliciously intimate. With exquisite restraint, his tongue glided along the rim of her lower lip, then, as she opened to him, slipped into her mouth to play with the tip of hers. His touch ignited a warm shimmer that flowed downward through Terri's body, heating like molten lava as it pooled in the deepest part of her. Her hands framed his head, fingers tangling in his hair as she pulled him down to deepen the kiss. Her body curled against his, hips pressing into an erection that was already big and hard.

He laughed mischievously, his lips moving down her throat to delve into the moist hollow between her breasts. "Take it easy, lady," he whispered. "We've got all night, and I plan to see that you enjoy every minute."

Not until Terri was in his arms did Buck realize how much he'd wanted her there. Something about the way her curves molded to his, her strength, her sweet, willing warmth, made him feel as if he'd come home. Holding her was as natural as breathing—

coupled with a rush that was like the first few seconds of free fall in an early-morning skydive. Lord, but she felt good.

He'd made love to her once before, and it had been wonderful. But it had been nowhere near enough.

"We're in the wrong place," he murmured against the fragrant curve of her neck. "Come on, I've got a better idea."

With a rough laugh he kissed her again, then caught her in his arms, swept her through the dark living room and half carried her up the stairs. They reached the landing and stood breathless for a moment, looking out the high window at the night sky. The storm was moving east, the clouds thinning to show patches of starry sky. "It's beautiful," Terry whispered.

"So are you." He nibbled the tip of her ear. "I've been wanting you all night—no way I could've just taken you home and let you go. But now..." His gaze swept the expanse of the sky. "We've got all night if we want."

Tossing aside his tux jacket, he tugged her down beside him on the top step, where they could sit in full view of the night sky above towering canyon walls. Under different conditions, this would be a good time to talk. But he knew better than to tell her what he was feeling. The words he needed to say would spoil this moment completely. The less said the better.

Pulling her close, he kissed her, going deep with his tongue. By now his blood was pounding and his erection was threatening to burst through a seam, but he willed himself not to hurry, not even when she responded with a moan and wiggled her hips closer.

His hand reached down and slid up her leg, half expecting to find pantyhose. But Terri's sleek, tanned legs were bare. The surprise kicked his pulse into overdrive. He kissed her again, sliding his hand up to the crotch of her panties. Her breath caught as he fingered the fabric, stroking her through the thin silk.

She arched upward to meet his hand. "Touch me," she whispered. "I want you to."

"I can do more than that," he muttered. Easing her back onto the landing he knelt two steps below her, slid her panties off her legs, hiked up the narrow part of her skirt and lowered his head.

"Oh—" She gasped in wonder as his tongue found the spot. "Nobody ever…did that to me…before…" She moaned as he savored the sweet-salty taste of her, feeling the tiny nub swell beneath his touch. Her fingers tangled in his hair as she swam in the new sensation. "That feels so…so…" The words trailed off as he brought her to a shuddering climax.

"Come here, you." She seized his shoulders, drawing him up for a lingering kiss. Seeing her like this, so warm and playful and eager, tugged at his heart. He would trade anything for the chance to pamper her, make her happy and give her everything her heart desired. Reason told him that chance was already gone. But at least they had tonight. He would make the most of it.

By now, all thought of taking it slow had evaporated. He wanted her—wanted her now, cloaking his sex in her hot, tight body, meeting his thrusts with her own. Standing, he pulled her to her feet. His hands ranged hungrily over her silk-clad curves, molding her breasts, pressing her hips in hard against him. She was equally eager as she tugged his shirt open. Her urgency sent buttons clattering to the floor and bouncing down the stairs.

Searching, his fingers found the zipper tab that opened her gown down the back. He gave it a firm tug. The zipper parted about eight inches, then stuck. He pulled again, then yanked. The zipper wouldn't budge.

She gazed up at him, mischief in her eyes and a smile teasing her luscious mouth. "Rip it," she said.

They left a trail of clothes and shoes all the way down the hall to the bedroom.

Buck opened his eyes. It was early yet, with sunrise casting a rosy glow through the shutters. Lying here with Terri in his arms, he felt physical contentment to the marrow of his bones. He'd had other women, more than he cared to remember, but never one who matched his desire the way Terri did. Last night had been more than sex. It had been as if their souls were making love.

He wanted to do it again, every night for as long as he lived. He wanted to build the kind of life she was leaving him to find—to give her children who'd be brothers and sisters for Quinn, to share adventures as a family, to love and support and cherish each other for all time.

But as the dawn faded from rose to gray, he knew the odds of that dream coming true were all but hopeless. He was in love with Terri, and he sensed that she loved him, too. But the secret of his past would always stand between them. Even if he never told her, the silent lie would be there, lurking like a hidden poison—and if she were to find out what he'd kept from her, she would never forgive him.

Propping his head on one arm, he gazed down at her. She was so lovely in the soft light, her rich chestnut hair framing her face in silky tendrils, her lashes like velvet fringe against her warmly freckled cheeks. The lips that had returned his kisses with so much passion were moist and ripely swollen. He ached to lean over, capture those lips and begin again where they'd left off. But she looked so peaceful in sleep, and waking her would mean getting up out of bed, pulling on some clothes, driving her home and saying goodbye, maybe forever.

He loved her. He wanted her for keeps. There had to be a way. Why couldn't he find it?

And then, suddenly, he knew.

He had to tell her the truth.

What were the odds that she'd hate him for it? Pretty damned high. And the fact that he'd kept it from her all these years would only make things worse. She'd probably leave and never speak to him again.

But if he wanted a life with her, he would have to take the chance and weather the consequences.

Terri was already aware that her brother had died from a sniper's bullet while on patrol. But telling her *why* would be one of the hardest things he'd ever done—and the biggest gamble he'd ever taken.

He would tell her this morning—but not here, in this bed, where they'd made love.

Warm and sleepy, she stirred beside him. Her eyelids fluttered open. "Hi," she murmured, smiling.

"Hi," he said. "You're a goddess when you're sleeping, did you know that?"

"Silly, how would I know?" She gave a little shake of her head as he leaned closer. "No kissing till I clean my teeth. I promise you won't like the taste of me."

He sat up. "I loved the taste of you last night. But if we start kissing, I'll never let you out of my bed, and we need to get the day started. What would you say to some breakfast?"

"Sounds good. But I don't have anything to wear."

Buck glanced down at her crumpled silk evening gown on the floor. It wouldn't be comfortable to put back on, even if he hadn't managed to break the zipper getting her out of it. "I've got some spare sweats," he said. "The bottoms have a drawstring, so they won't fall down on you—not that I'd mind."

Naked, he slipped out of bed and moved to his walk-in closet, where he found what he was looking for. Grabbing one set of sweats for himself, he tossed a second set onto the bed for her.

She laughed, watching him without a trace of embarrassment. "Oh, darn, you're getting dressed? I was just enjoying the view. Did anybody ever tell you how delectable you look from the rear?"

"You're shameless." Adoring her, he pulled on the sweatpants. He could tell she was already putting on a brave face, readying herself for the parting they both dreaded.

If nothing else, maybe what he had to tell her would make that parting easier.

"Go ahead and put yourself together," he said. "I'll be downstairs cooking you some bacon and eggs."

"And a big mug of coffee, please. I need it this morning."

"You've got it." He strolled out of the room and down the stairs, thinking how comfortable it was, being with Terri. He could be happy making breakfast for her every morning of their lives. But that wasn't something he could count on. He needed to prepare himself for the worst.

Downstairs, he went out back and checked on Murphy, giving the big mutt a morning ear scratch and refilling his water and kibble bowls. Then he came back inside, washed his hands, and started the bacon and coffee. From overhead, he could hear Terri running the guest room shower. He whistled as he worked, trying to take his mind off the urge to race upstairs and join her.

He was just adding grated cheddar to the scrambled eggs when she came downstairs, her face damp and glowing. She'd taken the braids and ribbon out of her hair, letting it hang loose around her shoulders. "All ready," he said, dishing up the eggs, then pulling out her chair. "Have a seat."

She sat. He poured coffee for both of them and took his seat across from her. She sipped her coffee, her copper-flecked eyes meeting his across the table. She looked so vulnerable, and now he was about to hurt her. Lord, how was he going to do this?

"I don't want you to leave," he said. "You know that, don't you?"

"You've made that clear." She glanced down at her breakfast, poking at her eggs as if she'd suddenly lost her appetite. "But my life hasn't changed in ten years. If I don't do something different, it never will."

"There's no reason your life couldn't change here, if you opened yourself to it." He was stumbling now, saying everything except what he'd planned to say.

"My mind's made up," she said. "If that job offer in Park City looks good, I'm taking it. It's time, Buck. I can't stay here any longer."

"Well then, I'll just have to respect your decision." He took a ragged breath, then plunged ahead. "Terri, there's something I've held back all these years because I didn't know how to tell you. Now that you're leaving, this may be my last chance to let you know how sorry I am."

She looked startled. Then her face took on a resolute expression. "I can't imagine what it would be. But if there's something you need to say, I'm listening."

"It's about Steve and how he died."

He glimpsed the look of pain that flickered across her face. Some wounds, he knew, never healed.

"You know he was shot," he said, "and you know he was carried back to camp, where he died. What you don't know is that what happened was my fault."

Her lips moved, shaping each word with effort. "What do you mean?"

Buck took a breath, then began the story he'd never told anyone before, not even Diane.

"Steve had gone on patrol the night before. He wasn't scheduled to go out the next morning. I was. But I woke up at dawn with a splitting migraine—I still get them, as you know."

"Yes, I know."

"But never as bad as the one I had that morning. I was so sick I was throwing up. I could barely see to get dressed, but I got my gear and suited up, determined to go anyway. Then somebody told our lieutenant. He looked me over and said I'd be useless out there if I couldn't see to shoot. He called for a volunteer to take my place."

"And Steve volunteered." Her voice was a whisper, drained of emotion. Her eyes were unreadable.

"That's right, and you know the rest. If I'd been in shape to go out on that patrol, or if I'd insisted on going anyway, even with a migraine, Steve would have survived that day. He'd very likely have come home, been here for you all along when your grandmother got sick, married, had children…" Buck's voice trailed off. "I could have toughed it out," he said. "I could have argued with the lieutenant, convinced him I'd be all right. Or better yet, I could have faked it and not told anybody. Maybe I would've been shot, or maybe things would've gone differently for me. Either way, Steve wouldn't have been the one to die that day."

She'd put down her fork. An eternity seemed to pass before she spoke. "You couldn't have known what would happen. Neither could Steve."

"But I knew the risks. Every time we went on patrol we were taking our lives in our hands." Buck struggled to keep the emotion out of his voice. "Later that morning, I was in camp, still wondering whether I'd done the right thing, when I heard the patrol come back. Somebody told me Steve was wounded. I got to him just in time to say goodbye."

Terri didn't speak. A single tear trickled down her face.

"Lord, Terri, I would've done anything to trade places with him. If it were possible right now, I'd change things so that I'd be the one lying in that grave and Steve would be here with you."

Terri's silence said more than any words she could have spoken. When she finally looked up at him, the coldness in her eyes told Buck he'd already lost her.

"I understand what happened," she said, "and I don't hold you responsible. What I don't understand is why you waited all these years to tell me."

It was a tough question, and the answer didn't come easily. "The very last thing Steve asked was that I take care of you. I promised him I'd do that. When I got home and saw how you were still hurting, I knew you were going to need my help. But I was afraid that if I told you the truth, you wouldn't want anything to do with me."

Her gaze hardened. "You should have given me that choice. Instead you treated me like a child."

"I know better now. I didn't then—and as time passed, it got harder and harder to bring it up. But I was wrong. You deserved to know. Forgive me, Terri. I tried to make it up to you over the years—"

"Make it up to me?" Her fist clenched on the table-top. "So you took me under your wing and gave me a job—out of *guilt*?" She rose, trembling. "You bought me new tires, bought flowers for my grandma and took me to the gala out of *guilt*? Did you sleep with me out of guilt, too?"

"Terri, I didn't mean—" he protested, but she cut him off.

"Never mind. Your excuses don't matter anymore. I've given you ten years of my life. That's enough. Take me home. I need to pack."

Buck knew better than to argue as he drove to her house. He'd gambled and he'd lost. Another word from him would only set loose more bottled-up anger. But as they pulled up to her house there was one thing he needed to ask.

"What should I tell Quinn?"

She looked directly at him for the first time since they'd left his house. Only then did Buck see the welling tears in her eyes. "Tell her I'm sorry, and that I'll be in touch. Maybe…" She paused, as if flustered. "Oh, never mind. Have a nice life, Buck."

Turning away, she climbed out of the vehicle. Still wearing his sweats and her muddy black pumps, she stalked into the house.

As the Hummer roared away from the house, Terri locked the door behind her, slid to the floor and buried her face against her knees. Her shoulders shook with sobs.

It was over. Really over. And after last night's love-making, letting go hurt even worse than she'd feared it would. She'd hoped, at least, for a sweet and tender farewell. But Buck's revelation over breakfast had made that impossible.

She could forgive him for letting Steve take his place on patrol—in fact, she already had. Steve had chosen to volunteer, and his death was a consequence of the war, a cruel twist of fate that hadn't been Buck's fault. Harder to forgive was the way he'd hidden the truth from her, keeping the secret for years, as if she were a child, incapable of understanding. But worst of all was the fact that any kindness he'd shown her had been motivated more by guilt and pity than by genuine caring. As for love…

But she wouldn't even go there. Buck had never even pretended to love her, and unrequited love was a one-way ticket to misery.

Time to move on. Terri pushed to her feet, stepped

out of her mud-stained pumps and padded into the bathroom to splash her face with water. Then she stripped off the sweats Buck had lent her, folded them neatly and put on her usual Sunday wear—jeans, sneakers and a faded T-shirt. The clean khaki uniforms she wore to work, with the Bucket List logo on the shirts, hung in her closet. Seized by an impulse, she yanked them off their hangers and tossed them on the bed. Then she folded each piece and stacked them next to the sweats. When Buck came to work Monday morning, he would find them on his desk, along with her ring of keys.

Her job interview was scheduled for Monday at ten thirty. She planned to make it a two-day trip, leaving here before noon and staying the night in Park City. Her overnight case should be enough to hold everything she needed. Packing wouldn't take long. Neither would dropping off the keys and uniforms in Buck's office. But her most important task would take more time and thought. She needed to write a letter—the most heart-wrenching letter she'd ever written.

Switching on her computer, she sat down at her desk, brought up the word processor and began to type.

Dear Quinn...

Buck had dreaded Monday morning, driving to work with Quinn, unlocking the door, knowing Terri wouldn't be there. He'd entertained the secret hope that he'd walk in and find her at her desk, her smile enough to tell him she'd changed her mind. But he should've known it wasn't to be. Stepping into his office, seeing the folded clothes and the keys she'd left for him slammed reality hard in his face.

Quinn came dragging in behind him. He'd managed to tell her last night that Terri was leaving. She wasn't taking the news well. When he handed her the envelope with her name written on the outside, she looked at it for a moment, then laid it on the desk and turned away.

"Aren't you going to open it?" he asked her.

She shook her head. "If you want to read it, you can open it yourself."

"You don't mind?" Maybe if he knew what the letter said, he could talk her into reading it. He knew she'd feel betrayed by Terri's leaving. But she wouldn't feel that way forever.

She shrugged. "Go ahead."

Buck tore open the envelope and unfolded the letter.

Dear Quinn,

I'm sorry I had to leave without saying goodbye. I should have told you sooner that I was planning to go, but I didn't want to spoil our good times together. In the end, things happened so fast that I ran out of time.

An ache tightened around Buck's heart. He'd had ten years to fall in love with Terri—ten years to win her and make her his. But he'd come to his senses too late. He, too, had run out of time. He read to the end of the letter.

I stayed in Porter Hollow to be with my grandmother. Now that she's gone, it's time for me to try new things in new places. By the time you read this, I'll be in Park City, negotiating a job there.

Thank you again, and please thank Ann Marie, too, for helping me get ready for the party. The gown and my hair looked beautiful. You'll be upset with me, I know, for leaving like this, but in time I hope you'll understand and forgive me, and that we'll always be friends. You have my phone number and email. I'm really hoping to hear from you.

Love always,

Terri

Buck turned to his daughter. "You should read this," he said. "At least it might help you understand why she went away."

Quinn took the letter, crumpled it in her small fist and flung it in the wastepaper basket.

Terri bought the home pregnancy test kit on the way to Park City, in a town where nobody knew her. She planned to wait until after the job interview to take the test. If she *was* pregnant, then she'd need maternity leave in a matter of months, which might be a deal breaker. She wanted to be as calm and as truthful as possible and, since she wouldn't know for sure, she'd be less tempted to lie.

But she should've known her penchant for honesty would trip her up. When the manager, a breezy, athletic woman in her forties, confirmed her interest in hiring her on the spot, Terri knew she had to tell the truth.

"There's a chance I may be pregnant," she said, her stomach fluttering as she spoke the word for the first time. "I'm not sure yet, but I wouldn't feel right about keeping it from you."

The woman lifted off her glasses and rubbed the bridge of her nose. "We should be able to work around that," she said. "Assuming you are pregnant and plan to keep the baby, I'm guessing you'd be due in the spring. That's our slow time, between the ski season and the summer events. Taking a couple of months off shouldn't be a problem, especially if you're willing to do some work from home. Just so you'll know, in the ten years I've worked here, I've had two babies myself." She replaced her glasses and smiled. "There's a vacant apartment in the complex where I live. We'd like you to start this weekend if you can manage it. Is that okay, or do you need more time?"

Thirty minutes later, feeling a bit giddy, Terri walked out of the resort headquarters with her new employment contract in her purse. She'd done it. She'd spread her wings and, so far, managed to stay airborne. It had happened so fast, her head was still spinning.

Her motel room was in nearby Heber City, outside the pricey ski district. She'd planned to start home this afternoon, but now that she had a job, it made more sense to stay an extra day, check out the area, and either reserve the apartment or find something else.

Her thoughts churned as she drove. It was time she summoned the courage to take the pregnancy test. If the result was negative, she'd be free to move on with her life. If it was positive, if she was really carrying Buck's child—

But she'd deal with that once she knew for sure. If there really was to be a baby, two things were already settled in her mind. First, she would keep it, love it, raise it. And second, she wouldn't tell Buck. The man had done enough for her out of guilt. The last thing she wanted was a repeat of his miserable shotgun marriage to Diane.

The pregnancy test was still in her purse. Pulling up to the motel, she parked the Jeep and went into her room. In the bathroom, with shaking hands, she opened the box and followed the instructions, then waited, her eyes glued to the indicator.

She counted her heartbeats as the seconds passed. Slowly the sign emerged—a small but unmistakable plus.

She was going to be a mother.

Eleven

Park City, Utah
December, six months later

Hi, Terri,
I'm glad we're still Facebook friends. I missed
you too much to stay mad forever. But I really
wish I could see you. I'm here in Sedona with
Mom, but I'll be spending Christmas vacation
with Dad in Porter Hollow. Maybe you can come
and visit us. Or we could come see you in Park
City. It would be fun to play in the snow. Do you
know how to ski yet? Maybe you could teach
me. We could have so much fun. Think about it.
XOXOXOX,
Quinn

Terri sighed as she reread Quinn's message. When Buck's daughter had contacted her from Sedona in September, she'd been happy about it. She truly loved Quinn and knew that her leaving had hurt the girl. Their Facebook exchanges had been harmless enough while Quinn was with her mother. But now Quinn would be with Buck, in Porter Hollow. And she'd be pushing her father to come to Park City for a visit.

Rising from her chair, Terri reached back and massaged the strain from her lower back. The baby—a healthy little boy—wasn't due till March. But she was already showing—not too much under a jacket or coat. But in her regular clothes, there was no hiding the bump. She wasn't huge yet, but she looked unmistakably pregnant. There was no way she could let Quinn or Buck see her. Having Buck find out she was pregnant would turn her whole carefully restructured life upside down. She couldn't let it happen. She needed to nip Quinn's plans in the bud—now.

Terri sat down again. Her fingers quivered on the keys as she wrote her reply.

Dear Quinn,
I'd love to see you, but the Christmas holiday season is our busiest time here in Park City. If you and your dad were to come, I wouldn't have any time to be with you, and you'd be lucky to find a place to stay. With so much going on here, I can't get away to visit Porter Hollow. Maybe we can make it some other time.
Hugs,
Terri

She clicked the enter key with a deep sense of misgiving. Everything she'd written was true, except the one big lie of omission. If she wanted to keep her baby a secret, there could be no *some other time.* Not ever.

If she'd had the foresight to think this out, she might have gone somewhere farther away where she could have cut off all communication with her past. But there were practicalities to consider. The severance payments she'd elected to have paid out monthly were going directly to her bank account, which meant that Buck had to have some idea where she was. And some issues with the sale of her grandmother's property were still being negotiated so the Realtor needed to be in touch with her, as well.

But it struck her, in a sudden flash of insight, that there was more than practicality involved here. There was Quinn—sweet, blameless Quinn who loved her; Quinn who, if the secret was kept, would never know she had a baby brother. And there was her unborn son who would never know his father and his wonderful big sister.

The truth hit her so hard that she gasped out loud.

What gave her the right to play with these innocent children's lives—to deny them the joy and support of knowing each other—for the sake of her own pride?

Terri buried her face in her hands. What had she done? How could she fix this mess without wrecking Buck's life and her own?

It was coming up on five o'clock when Evie Redfeather dropped Quinn off at Buck's office. Alerted by a phone call, Buck was waiting outside when Evie's Buick pulled up to the curb. When the door opened, Quinn came flying out and hurtled into his arms. He grabbed her tight, swinging off her feet.

"Hey, you're getting tall!" he exclaimed, setting her down and heading for the open truck to get her suitcase.

"I know. I'm the tallest girl in my class. What're we going to do while I'm here?"

Buck waved his thanks to Evie as she pulled away and headed home. "What do you say we talk about it over pizza at Giovanni's?" he asked, hefting her suitcase and taking her hand. He'd learned some lessons about being a father last summer. Those lessons were paying off. It surprised and delighted him how much closer he and his daughter had grown.

"Can we have hot fudge sundaes afterward?" she asked, matching his stride.

"Sure." Buck remembered last summer when Terri had gone for pizza with them. The empty spot her departure had left still ached. He'd hoped to hear from her, but she hadn't called or emailed even once. He could only respect her choice and hope she was doing all right.

Even in December, the weather in Porter Hollow was mild enough for their light jackets. Stowing the suitcase in the Hummer, they walked the short distance to the restaurant. The pretty blonde waitress showed them to a booth. Her body language made it clear that she was interested. But Buck's mind was elsewhere, especially now, with his daughter along.

"So, what's new?" he asked her as they faced each other across the red-checked tablecloth.

"Oh, a few things." Quinn sipped her root beer.

"Like what?"

"Mom's got a boyfriend. He's kind of a jerk, but he's got lots of money. I think they're getting married."

"You're kidding." Diane had had plenty of men in her life since the end of their marriage, but none who could talk her into giving up that fat alimony check he put in her account every month.

"His family owns some factories in China. They make underwear or car-seat covers or something like that. Anyway, they've got this big house in Switzerland—that's where they keep all their money. He said something about being neighbors to George Clooney."

A dark weight formed in the pit of Buck's stomach. What would he do if Diane married and wanted to take their daughter out of the country, maybe put her in some snooty Swiss boarding school? Could he fight it legally and win?

"Mom wanted me to ask you something," Quinn said.

"Okay." Buck braced himself for bad news.

"If she gets married, she wants to know if I could live with you during the school year and go to school here in Porter Hollow. Then I could visit her in the summer, like I visit you now."

Buck began to breathe again. "I'd like that a lot." He hesitated. "Would you?"

"You bet I would." She grinned and held up her hand for a high five.

Soon after that their pizza arrived. Quinn wolfed down two slices, then suddenly gave her father a serious look. "What if you get married, too?" she asked. "Would you ship me off to Switzerland to be with Mom?"

"No way. We'd all be family together, or it wouldn't happen. But I don't think you have much to worry about. Do you see any women lining up to marry me?"

She stirred the ice in her root beer. "I always kind of hoped you'd marry Terri."

"To tell you the truth, I was kind of hoping the same thing. But it wasn't in the cards."

"Did you ask her?" Quinn demanded.

Buck shook his head. "I never got that far. She was mad at me when she left. I'm guessing she still is. I haven't had so much as a Tweet from her."

Quinn swirled her ice a moment before she met his gaze. "She's not mad at me, Dad. We've been emailing back and forth since this fall, when I went back to Mom's."

Buck's pulse skipped. "How is she? Is she all right?"

"She's fine. She likes her new job. She's asked me about you a couple of times."

"Asked what?"

"Oh, just stuff like whether you were okay, and had

you found anybody to take her job. I told her you still just had Bob and the temps."

"Do you think she wants to come back?"

"I asked her. She said no."

"Has she met anybody? Is she dating?" Buck could've smacked the side of his own head for asking. If the answer was yes, did he really want to know?

"Not anybody that she's said. But she'd tell stuff like that to a grown-up girlfriend, not to me." Quinn gave him a thoughtful look. "You really like her, don't you, Dad?"

"I guess I do." Buck fished for his credit card to pay the check. "But I also guess it doesn't make much difference whether I like her or not. Terri's moved on. She's not coming back here."

Quinn dawdled, finishing the last of her root beer. She seemed to be holding something back.

"We could go see her," she said. "I already asked her if we could come, and she said she was too busy. But if we just showed up, she'd have to see us, wouldn't she?"

Buck signed the check and pocketed his card. "I don't know if that's a good idea," he said. "What if Terri doesn't want to see us?"

"Then we could just have some fun by ourselves and go home. At least we'd know she was all right."

"Why wouldn't she be all right?" Buck shrugged into his leather jacket. Quinn had always been a perceptive child, an old soul, as her mother called her. Maybe her instincts were telling her something. "Do you have some reason to be worried about Terri?" he asked.

Quinn walked ahead of him through the door, waiting outside for him to catch up. "I just wonder why she wouldn't want to see me. Terri's my friend. She likes me. What if something's wrong?"

"Maybe I'm the one she doesn't want to see."

Quinn had no reply for that. But as they went for sundaes and drove home, Buck couldn't stop turning the thought over in his mind. He'd tried to tell himself that letting Terri move on was the fairest thing he could do for her. But letting her go had been like ripping away a vital part of himself.

So help him, he still loved her. And now that Quinn had planted the worry in his mind, Buck knew he wouldn't rest until he saw Terri and made sure she was safe, happy and where she wanted to be.

Terri assembled the packets she'd prepared for the quarterly board of directors meeting and placed them around the table in the conference room. Her mind checked off the mental list she'd made—snacks, chilled water and sodas, napkins, pens, notepads, whiteboard markers and erasers, a computer to run the presentation on the wall-mounted TV—everything a roomful of important people would need for three hours of debate and decision making.

The meeting wouldn't start till after lunch, but there was nothing like being prepared ahead of time. Ginetta, her boss, would be running the meeting. With the setup complete, Terri's job was done. Good thing, because she was getting tired, and the baby was kicking like a little ninja.

"Everything looks great." Ginetta surveyed the room, then gave Terri a concerned glance. "You look like you could use a rest. Why don't you go in the break room and stretch out on the couch? It'll do you a world of good."

"Thanks, but it's almost noon. I won't get much rest in there, with people coming in to eat their lunch. Anyway, I promised myself I'd write up that order for cleaning supplies and send it out. As long as I can sit at my desk, I'll be fine."

"At least go get yourself a nice lunch." Ginetta slipped off her glasses and rubbed the bridge of her nose. "You've been here six months. You're doing a fine job, but all I've seen you do is work. You come in early, stay till all hours… You need to get out and make some friends. Have some fun."

"Maybe later. For now, I have the baby to think of." Terri crossed the common area to her small office and sat down at her desk. It felt good to take the weight off her feet.

Ginetta followed her to stand by the desk. "Forgive me if this is too personal, Terri. I'm just concerned. Will you have anybody to help you when the baby comes? What about your family?"

"No family. I'm the last one."

"What about your baby's father? Is he in the picture?"

Terri shook her head. "He doesn't know."

"Married?" She paused, catching herself. "I'm sorry, that's none of my business."

"No, he's not married. It's…complicated."

Ginetta touched her shoulder. "Well, let me know if there's anything I can do to help—and you really do need to take better care of yourself."

As her boss walked out of the office, Terri rested her eyes a moment, then turned to her computer and brought up the ordering form for the resort's janitorial supplies. She was lucky to have a boss as understanding as Ginetta. But until she decided how to resolve her baby's future, the fewer people she involved in her problems, the better.

She was partway down the form when her cell phone rang. She reached into her purse, grabbed the phone and, without taking time to check the ID, answered the call.

"Hi, Terri! This is Quinn!" The girlish voice sounded happy, excited. At least Terri could surmise that nothing was wrong.

"Hi, Quinn. What's up?" Terri kept her tone light and cheerful.

"I'm here in Park City, with Dad. Evie flew us in the jet. We wanted to surprise you. Wait a sec, I'll put Dad on."

Terri's heart sank like a drowning butterfly. She'd made the decision to break her news when the time was right—maybe with a well-thought-out phone call or email to Buck. But now was too soon. She needed to think things through. What could she say to Buck? And how could she explain to a nine-year-old girl how she'd come to be pregnant with her father's baby? Quinn was precocious, but surely the child wasn't ready to hear that.

"Hello, Terri." Buck's voice went through her with the hot pain of memory. "How're you doing?"

"Fine." Terri struggled to keep her voice from shaking. "I wish you'd let me know you were coming. I'm having an extremely busy day. I won't even have time to—"

"Just have lunch with us. If that's all you've got time for, we'll understand."

Terri thought fast, scrambling for an exit strategy. Now that they were here, she knew there was no way Quinn and Buck would leave without seeing her, at least for lunch. But if she kept her coat on while she was with them, maybe they wouldn't notice the change in her body.

"I guess I could manage that," she said. "On the second floor of the hotel across the street from my office, there's an outdoor restaurant with a view of the slopes. It's a nice day, and Quinn might enjoy watching the skiers while we eat. There's a stairway going up from the street. If you're close by, you can't miss it. How soon can you meet me there?"

"We're on Main Street now," Buck said. "I can see the stairway to the restaurant from here. We'll be there in a few minutes."

"I'm on my way." Heart pounding, Terri ended the

call and reached for the quilted, thigh-length down parka she'd bought in town. The coat was puffy enough to camouflage her pregnancy. The tougher challenge, she knew, would be masking her emotions.

Buck ushered his excited daughter up the snow-packed stairs to the restaurant. Quinn had seen winter weather before, but not for a few years. On their way to the stairs, she'd scooped up handfuls of snow, shaping the white stuff into balls and laughing as she tossed them in the air. Once Terri would have dropped everything to play with her. Now she claimed she was too busy. Something had changed. What was it?

The restaurant was crowded, with a long waiting line, but a generous tip got Buck quickly seated at a good table with a view. Outdoor heaters, placed among the tables, warmed the air, but it was still chilly. He ordered hot cocoa for Quinn while they waited for Terri to arrive.

A few minutes later she came up the stairs, wearing a bulky dark green parka and holding tightly to the rail. Her face was flushed, her expression harried. But she smiled when she spotted Buck and Quinn, who was waving her over to their table.

Buck stood to pull out her chair. Sitting, she reached across the table and squeezed Quinn's hand. "Great to see you," she said. "How do you like the snow, Quinn?"

"I love it!" Quinn grinned. "I wish we could stay long enough for me to take ski lessons. I want to do what those people are doing." She indicated the slopes with a sweep of her hand. "Have you learned how to ski yet, Terri?"

"I've been too busy working," Terri said. "Maybe next year."

Buck studied her across the table. Terri was smiling, chatting with Quinn. But she looked tired. And the way she'd come up the stairs, gripping the rail as if pulling herself up. Was something wrong, or was worry feeding his imagination?

They ordered tuna melts and hot soup. Buck noticed how Terri picked at her food, as if too nervous to eat. Was it because he and Quinn were here, or was something else bothering her?

"Are you all right, Terri?" he asked. "You look a little frayed around the edges."

"I'm fine. Just stressed. I like my job, but this is the busy season—lots to do. And I haven't been sleeping well, probably too much coffee." She made a show of glancing at her watch. "I can't stay long—just wanted to say hello and catch up." She turned away from him. "How do you like school this year, Quinn? Tell me about your classes."

She was making small talk—avoiding him, Buck could tell. After their parting he could hardly blame her for being uncomfortable. But he was seeing more than that. This wasn't the breezy, confident Terri he remembered. She was like a wild bird, ready to take flight if he so much as reached out a hand to her.

Only one thing was solid in his mind. He loved

her more deeply than ever. But he was growing more concerned by the minute. Something was troubling her. Something bigger than their unexpected visit. How could he leave her without knowing what it was?

She finished her soup, having barely nibbled the sandwich, and glanced at her watch again. "Oh, dear, I really need to be going now. I've got so much happening at work." She rose, motioning Buck to stay seated as he shifted his chair back. "Please don't bother getting up. You should stay and order some dessert. The cheesecake here is pure heaven. So good to see you both. Say hi to Evie for me, and enjoy the rest of your day."

She blew a departing kiss to Quinn, turned away and fled like an escaping prisoner toward the stairs. Buck watched her go. He needed to talk to her again—alone this time, he resolved. Maybe he could call her later, or even stay an extra day and try to see her again tonight.

His gaze followed the back of her dark green coat as she wove her way through the crowd. Something in him wanted to rush after her and stop her from leaving. He curbed the impulse. If Terri wanted to run away, he had no right to interfere.

What happened next happened fast. Two rough-housing teenage boys were wrestling each other in the waiting line. Grabbing and shoving, they stumbled hard against Terri, who'd just reached the top of the stairs and taken the first step down. The impact knocked her off balance. Arms flailing, she pitched forward, cried out and disappeared from Buck's sight.

A collective gasp went up from the watchers. Buck shot out of his seat and bulled his way through the crowd to the top of the stairs. Looking down, he could see Terri at the bottom. She lay sprawled faceup on the icy sidewalk, her eyes closed.

In an instant he was at her side. He didn't dare lift or move her, but as he touched her cheek, her eyelids fluttered open. Her lips moved as she struggled to speak.

"Get me to the hospital," she said.

"I've called nine-one-one," a man standing nearby told Buck. "They're sending an ambulance."

"Thanks." Buck held Terri's cold hand. "Lie still," he murmured. "Help's on its way, and I'm here. I love you, Terri. Do you hear me? You're going to be fine."

She didn't speak, but her fingers tightened around his.

Somehow, in the confusion, Quinn had found her way down the stairs to crouch beside him. Her eyes were huge and scared in her small, pale face.

"Will Terri be all right, Daddy?" she asked.

Buck laid his free hand on her shoulder. "Let's hope so. But if you want to say a little prayer, that couldn't hurt."

Quinn bowed her head, her lips moving in a whispered prayer. By the time she'd finished, the ambulance was pulling up to the curb. The paramedics supported Terri's neck and back, eased her onto a stretcher and loaded her into the vehicle. As it sped away, lights flashing, Buck and Quinn raced down the block to where they'd left their rental car.

Minutes later, they arrived at the hospital. By the time Buck checked at the emergency desk, Terri had been taken back to an examination room.

"Are you family?" the desk nurse asked.

"We're the closest thing to family she's got," Buck said, and realized it was true.

"Have a seat, the doctor will be out to talk to you after he's examined her." She turned away to answer a ringing phone.

Buck and Quinn settled on the couch to wait. Time crawled. Sick with worry, Buck thumbed through a stack of tattered magazines, barely aware of what he was seeing. Quinn asked for a dollar to get a soda from the vending machine. She came back and plopped down beside him. "Do you know what I think?" she asked.

"What?"

She popped the tab on her soda can. "I think you should ask Terri to marry you. We need her, and right now she needs us."

Buck smiled at her through his worry. "I think you're right. But what if she says no?"

"Then I'll talk her into it. I can talk Terri into anything."

Just then the doctor, a tall, balding man with glasses, came out into the waiting room. In an instant Buck was on his feet. He motioned the doctor into a side hall, out of Quinn's hearing. "How is she?" he asked, bracing for the worst.

"She's one very lucky lady," the doctor said. "That was a nasty fall she took. She's got a sprained wrist and some bruising, but no broken bones. And the baby appears to be fine."

"The baby?" Buck stared at the doctor, trying not to look like a fool. The last thing he'd expected was that Terri would be pregnant, but it all made sense now—the puffy coat, the nervous behavior. She hadn't wanted him to know. And it didn't take a genius to figure out why.

"We did a sonogram to make sure there was no problem," the doctor said. "Everything looked fine, but we'd like to keep her overnight for observation."

"Can I see her?"

"For a few minutes. Your little girl will have to wait out here. The nurse can keep an eye on her."

Buck thanked the doctor and walked back to where Quinn stood. "Terri's going to be all right," he said. "I'm going back to see her. You'll need to stay here. I won't be long. Okay?"

"Okay," Quinn said. "Are you going to ask her?"

"I'll see how it goes. See you in a few minutes." He turned to walk away.

"Dad—"

He glanced back at her. "What is it?"

"You can be pretty dense sometimes. Don't let her get away again."

"Got it." He flashed her a grin, which faded as

he strode back through the swinging doors. Quinn's view of the situation was simple—just ask her and don't give up till she says yes. But there were things Quinn didn't know, or was too young to understand.

He found Terri sitting up in bed, dressed in a hospital gown with a flannel blanket over her legs. Her right wrist was bandaged, and an IV with a saline drip was attached to her left arm. She looked pale and shaken, but otherwise all right.

Buck's first sight of her roused a storm of emotions—relief, outrage and a love so overpowering that it left him weak in the knees. Terri was the love of his life, the mother of his child. And he was mad enough to shake her silly.

He sank onto a chair that had been left next to the bed.

"You could've told me," he said.

"I know. I'd planned to tell you eventually. But I didn't want you thinking you had to do the right thing again. I saw what you went through with Diane, remember?"

"Blast it, Terri—" Buck bit back the rest of what wanted to be an angry outburst. That fall she'd taken could have killed both her and their child. But she was here, she was all right, and so was the baby. Anything—everything—else could be fixed.

"Listen to me." He reached across the bed and captured her hand in his. "We aren't perfect people, you and I. We've both done things that need forgiving—especially me. But damn it, I love you, Terri. Baby or no baby, I want to marry you and make a family—and Quinn wants it, too. So stop making excuses. Just say yes and make me the happiest man in the world."

Her gaze dropped to their clasped hands. He could imagine what was going through her mind. Was he proposing because of the baby? After the callous way he'd treated her in the past, could she really believe his claim that he loved her? Buck waited in an agony of hope and dread before she finally spoke.

"Do you really think we can make this work?" she asked.

Buck began to breathe again. She hadn't said no. There was still a chance. "We've been making it work for ten years," he said. "We just need to make some changes. You won't be my right-hand woman anymore. You'll be my center, my heart."

"Then, yes."

Buck wanted to shout with happiness. He wanted to turn cartwheels down the hall. But this was a hospital. He stood, leaned over her the bed and gave her a gently lingering kiss. "They're going to throw me out of here any minute," he said. "But when I come back here tomorrow I want to bring a ring and put it on your finger—or would you rather wait and pick one out yourself?"

"I have an idea," she said. "Take Quinn with you. Let her pick it out. Whatever she chooses will be perfect."

Buck barely had time for another kiss before the nurse appeared to usher him back to the waiting room. When she saw his face, Quinn broke into a wide smile.

"She said yes, didn't she, Daddy?"

"She did." Buck grabbed her hand. "Come on, young lady. You and I are going ring shopping."

Epilogue

Christmas Eve, one year later

Snow was falling, feathery light, on the big house in the canyon. Winter storms were rare in this warm country, and the snow seldom lasted long. Since this was Christmas Eve, the gentle storm added a special magic to the night.

As the clock struck eleven, Buck stood with Terri at the darkened window, watching the flakes drift down. Behind them, embers crackled in the fireplace where four stockings—one very small—hung from the mantel. A tall Christmas tree in the far corner glowed with light.

The two of them had put the children to bed and spent the past hour wrapping the last of the gifts.

Now they were tired, but the peace and beauty of the snow kept them lingering at the window. Buck slid his arms around his wife, cradling her against him in the glowing darkness. Her head rested in the hollow of his throat.

"Do you think Quinn will know what her present is when she opens that big box?" Terri asked.

Buck laughed. "When she sees that saddle and bridle, she'll figure it out. It's not like we can put her horse under the Christmas tree."

Quinn had been begging for a horse for months. Buck had bought her a well-broken registered mare and arranged to board it at a nearby stable. Terri had bought her a hat and some riding boots, now wrapped in another beribboned box.

"At least Stevie's easy this year," Terri said. "I bought him some clothes and a few little toys, but he'd be just as happy playing with boxes and ribbons."

"Or climbing up the stairs," Buck added.

At nine months, young Stevie Morgan was all boy. He hadn't started walking yet, but he could crawl like a little champ, and he was into everything. His latest fascination was the staircase, which he could already climb. Buck had added gates at the foot and top of the stairs, but it took everybody's vigilance to make sure the little explorer was safe. Quinn adored her baby brother, and she'd already become his favorite person.

Buck nuzzled his wife's ear, inhaling her womanly fragrance. Desire warmed inside him. He slid his hands upward, cradling her breasts through her silky shirt. "Maybe it's time we were in bed, too," he murmured. "Santa won't come if we're awake, you know."

She made a little purring sound. "Fine. But let's check the children on our way."

Holding hands, they mounted the stairs to the second-floor landing. Quinn's room was closest. Their daughter lay curled in sleep. Her walls were decorated with horse posters. She was growing up too fast, Buck thought. In no time at all she'd be a young woman. Every day of her childhood had become precious to him.

The nursery was across the hall from the master bedroom. Stevie sprawled in his crib, restless even in his sleep. With his mother's chestnut hair and his father's blue eyes, he was the baby they'd created the very first time they'd made love. Now Buck couldn't imagine life without him.

"We should make more of those," he whispered to Terri.

"Shhh…" She drew him out into the hallway and stretched on tiptoe to kiss him. "Bedtime," she whispered. "Come on."

Content to the marrow of his bones, he followed her into their bedroom.

* * * * *

Pick up all the Harlequin Desire novels from Elizabeth Lane

IN HIS BROTHER'S PLACE
THE SANTANA HEIR
THE NANNY'S SECRET
A SINFUL SEDUCTION
STRANDED WITH THE BOSS

***

If you're on Twitter, tell us what you think of Harlequin Desire! #harlequindesire

COMING NEXT MONTH FROM

HARLEQUIN *Desire*

Available August 9, 2016

#2461 FOR BABY'S SAKE
Billionaires and Babies • by Janice Maynard
Lila Baxter is all business. That's why she and easygoing
James Kavanagh broke off their relationship. But when she
unexpectedly inherits a baby, she'll have to face him again...and he
might win it all this time.

#2462 AN HEIR FOR THE BILLIONAIRE
Dynasties: The Newports • by Kat Cantrell
When single mother Nora O'Malley stumbles into the reclusive life of
her childhood best friend, he'll have to confront his dark past, and put
love before business, if he's ever to find happiness with her little family...

#2463 PREGNANT BY THE MAVERICK MILLIONAIRE
From Mavericks to Married • by Joss Wood
When former hockey player turned team CEO finds out his fling with a
determinedly single matchmaker has led to unexpected consequences,
he insists he'll be part of her life from now on...for the baby's sake, of
course!

#2464 CONTRACT WEDDING, EXPECTANT BRIDE
Courtesan Brides • by Yvonne Lindsay
If King Rocco does not have a bride and heir in a year's time, an ancient
law will force him to relinquish all power to the enemy. Courtesan
Ottavia Romolo might be the solution, but she demands his heart, too...

#2465 THE CEO DADDY NEXT DOOR
by Karen Booth
CEO and single father Marcus Chambers will only date women who
would be suitable mothers for his young daughter, but when his
free-spirited neighbor temporarily moves in after a fire destroys her
apartment, he finds himself falling for the worst possible candidate!

#2466 WAKING UP WITH THE BOSS
by Sheri WhiteFeather
Billionaire playboy Jake expected the fling with his personal assistant,
Carol, to be one and done. But when a surprise pregnancy brings them
closer, will it make this all-business boss want more than the bottom
line?

HDCNM0716

REQUEST YOUR FREE BOOKS!
2 FREE NOVELS PLUS 2 FREE GIFTS!

(H) HARLEQUIN®

Desire

ALWAYS POWERFUL, PASSIONATE AND PROVOCATIVE

YES! Please send me 2 FREE Harlequin® Desire novels and my 2 FREE gifts (gifts are worth about $10). After receiving them, if I don't wish to receive any more books, I can return the shipping statement marked "cancel." If I don't cancel, I will receive 6 brand-new novels every month and be billed just $4.55 per book in the U.S. or $5.24 per book in Canada. That's a savings of at least 13% off the cover price! It's quite a bargain! Shipping and handling is just 50¢ per book in the U.S. and 75¢ per book in Canada.* I understand that accepting the 2 free books and gifts places me under no obligation to buy anything. I can always return a shipment and cancel at any time. Even if I never buy another book, the two free books and gifts are mine to keep forever.

225/326 HDN GH2P

Name _____ (PLEASE PRINT) _____

Address _____ Apt. # _____

City _____ State/Prov. _____ Zip/Postal Code _____

Signature (if under 18, a parent or guardian must sign)

Mail to the **Reader Service:**
IN U.S.A.: P.O. Box 1867, Buffalo, NY 14240-1867
IN CANADA: P.O. Box 609, Fort Erie, Ontario L2A 5X3

Want to try two free books from another line?
Call 1-800-873-8635 or visit www.ReaderService.com.

* Terms and prices subject to change without notice. Prices do not include applicable taxes. Sales tax applicable in N.Y. Canadian residents will be charged applicable taxes. Offer not valid in Quebec. This offer is limited to one order per household. Not valid for current subscribers to Harlequin Desire books. All orders subject to credit approval. Credit or debit balances in a customer's account(s) may be offset by any other outstanding balance owed by or to the customer. Please allow 4 to 6 weeks for delivery. Offer available while quantities last.

Your Privacy—The Reader Service is committed to protecting your privacy. Our Privacy Policy is available online at www.ReaderService.com or upon request from the Reader Service.

We make a portion of our mailing list available to reputable third parties that offer products we believe may interest you. If you prefer that we not exchange your name with third parties, or if you wish to clarify or modify your communication preferences, please visit us at www.ReaderService.com/consumerchoice or write to us at Reader Service Preference Service, P.O. Box 9062, Buffalo, NY 14240-9062. Include your complete name and address.

HDI5

*Lila Baxter is all business. That's why she and easygoing
James Kavanagh broke off their relationship. But when
she unexpectedly inherits a baby, she'll have to face him
again…and he might win it all this time.*

Read on for a sneak peek of
FOR BABY'S SAKE, the latest installment in the
KAVANAGHS OF SILVER GLEN series
by USA TODAY *bestselling author*
Janice Maynard.

James Kavanagh liked working with his hands. Unlike his
eldest brother, Liam, who spent his days wearing an Italian
tailored suit, James was most comfortable in old jeans
and T-shirts. Truth be told, it was a good disguise. No one
expected a rich man to look like a guy who labored for a
paycheck.

That was fine with James. He didn't need people sucking
up to him because he was a Kavanagh. He wanted to be
judged on his own merits.

At the end of the day, a man was only as rich as his
reputation.

As he dipped his paintbrush into the can balanced on the
top of the ladder, he saw movement at the house next door.
Lila's house. A house he'd once known all too well.

It didn't matter. He was over her. Completely. The two of
them had been a fire that burned hot and bright, leaving only
ashes. It was for the best. Lila was too uptight, too driven,
too everything.

Still, something was going on. Lila's silver Subaru was parked in its usual spot. But it was far too early for her to be arriving home from work. He gave up the pretense of painting and watched as she got out of the car.

She was tall and curvy and had long blond curls that no amount of hair spray could tame. Lila had the body of a pinup girl and the brains of an accountant, a lethal combo. Then came his second clue that things were out of kilter. Lila was wearing jeans and a windbreaker. On a Monday.

He could have ignored all of that. Honestly, he was fine with the status quo. Lila had her job as vice president of the local bank, and James had the pleasure of dating women who were uncomplicated.

As he watched, Lila closed the driver's door and opened the door to the backseat. Leaning in, she gave him a tantalizing view of a nicely rounded ass. He'd always had a thing for butts. Lila's was first-class.

Suddenly, all thoughts of butts and sex and his long-ago love affair with his frustrating neighbor flew out the window. Because when Lila straightened, she was holding a baby.

Don't miss FOR BABY'S SAKE
by USA TODAY *bestselling author Janice Maynard.*
Available August 2016!

And meet all the Kavanagh brothers in the
***KAVANAGHS OF SILVER GLEN** series—*
In the mountains of North Carolina, one family discovers
that wealth means nothing without love.

A NOT-SO-INNOCENT SEDUCTION
BABY FOR KEEPS
CHRISTMAS IN THE BILLIONAIRE'S BED
TWINS ON THE WAY
SECOND CHANCE WITH THE BILLIONAIRE
HOW TO SLEEP WITH THE BOSS
FOR BABY'S SAKE

www.Harlequin.com

HDEXP0716

Whatever You're Into… Passionate Reads

Looking for more passionate reads from Harlequin®?
Fear not! Harlequin® Presents, Harlequin® Desire and
Harlequin® Blaze offer you irresistible romance stories
featuring powerful heroes.

◆HARLEQUIN *Presents.*

Do you want alpha males, decadent glamour and jet-set
lifestyles? Step into the sensational, sophisticated world of
Harlequin® Presents, where sinfully tempting heroes ignite a
fierce and wickedly irresistible passion!

◆HARLEQUIN *Desire*

Harlequin® Desire novels are powerful, passionate and
provocative contemporary romances set against a backdrop of
wealth, privilege and sweeping family saga. Alpha heroes with
a soft side meet strong-willed but vulnerable heroines amid a
dramatic world of divided loyalties, high-stakes conflict and
intense emotion.

◆HARLEQUIN *Blaze*

Harlequin® Blaze stories sizzle with strong heroines and
irresistible heroes playing the game of modern love and lust.
They're fun, sexy and always steamy.

Be sure to check out our full selection of books
within each series every month!

www.Harlequin.com

HPASSION2016

Turn your love of reading into
rewards you'll love with
Harlequin My Rewards

**Join for FREE today at
www.HarlequinMyRewards.com**

Earn **FREE BOOKS** of your choice.

Experience **EXCLUSIVE OFFERS** and contests.

Enjoy **BOOK RECOMMENDATIONS**
selected just for you.

PLUS! Sign up now
and get **500** points
right away!

Earn
FREE
REWARDS
HarlequinMyRewards.com
Join
Today!

MYR16R

HARLEQUIN®

A *Romance* FOR EVERY MOOD™

Love the Harlequin book you just read?

Your opinion matters.

Review this book on your favorite book site, review site, blog or your own social media properties and share your opinion with other readers!